REMINISCE
Unexpected moments open the path of eternal memories.

ARATI KOKANE

BLUEROSE PUBLISHERS
India | U.K.

Copyright © Arati Kokane 2024

All rights reserved by author. No part of this publication may be reproduced, stored in a retrieval system or transmitted in any form or by any means, electronic, mechanical, photocopying, recording or otherwise, without the prior permission of the author. Although every precaution has been taken to verify the accuracy of the information contained herein, the publisher assumes no responsibility for any errors or omissions. No liability is assumed for damages that may result from the use of information contained within.

BlueRose Publishers takes no responsibility for any damages, losses, or liabilities that may arise from the use or misuse of the information, products, or services provided in this publication.

For permissions requests or inquiries regarding this publication, please contact:

BLUEROSE PUBLISHERS
www.BlueRoseONE.com
info@bluerosepublishers.com
+91 8882 898 898
+4407342408967

ISBN: 978-93-5989-221-4

Cover Design: Sadhna Kumari
Typesetting: Pooja Sharma

First Edition: June 2024

Acknowlegement

To my parents mom Aparna and dad late Shri Dilip Vinayak Kelkar.

I am very greatful to my husband Rajiv who encouraged me to publish this book, who stressed on to get this book published. Without his backing it might not have happened.

I also want to show my heartiest gratituteds to my son Yash who encouraged me to write this book in first place. Who guided my on every step when I struggled, who also help me a lot through the ending of this book.

Through the medium of this book I would love to thank all my loved ones who are my support system throughout my life.

Preface

One morning I got up from my dream and I was literally shocked to have such a dream. It was not something usual. I was just thinking about the dream while finishing morning chores. To see I lost in my thoughts my husband asked about my lost face and then I told him about my dream. In my dream, I woke up and went in bathroom and see myself in the mirror. I looked a bit older than what I remember. Then suddently my husband was behaving very differently. When I went in my son's room, he is also grown up from what I remembered. And then afterwords I was told that that I have lost memory of some of my past years. After narrating this dream to my husband, this dream kept lingering in my mind for quite a while. One day I thought, this can be turned into a good story. So I started working on it. After giving lots and lots of twists and turns and changes I was able to give justice to my dream. And it finally took avatar in the form of this book.

Eventualy I understood one important thing that if I narrate my dream the next day (whatever I remember) it helps me to remember it for longer time. There are now so many stories to tell at my end. I hope to turn them into books in near future.

Contents

The Accident 1

Life Back to Normal…? 33

Where it started 57

The Beginning 81

Difficult Times 101

The New Normal 111

Reminisce 141

The Accident

"Ok. OK. Will meet you there by 8 o'clock" Mia assured on phone.

Mia started thinking quickly while getting ready for the meeting. 'Tanreja wants to meet today to finalize on designs instead of tomorrow as he is going to Delhi. This is so eleventh hour notice. It will take more than an hour to reach to his office. Don't know how long the meeting will last. If meeting lasts say maximum for two hours, as today we are taking final decisions on designs as well as media that means I wouldn't be able to reach home before eleven. Neelu is also on leave. That arises a question for dinner? Neil is at home. He will be hungry by the time I will reach home. This is so frustrating, but do I have a choice. The business is just started to catching up and it's not wise to give some lame excuses to Tanreja. He might be one of the major client. Only way is to order food before leaving, at least for Neil.

Mia decided to wear white kurta with white pants and peacock green dupatta for today's meeting. Mia is a beautiful young woman in her early 30s, with big eyes, fair complexion and wavy hairs. When she smiles, she smiles with her heart and eyes just lit up with that smile enhancing her beauty beyond explanation. Being a designer she has an eye for every beautiful aspects. She dresses perfectly for every occasion never under or overdressed. Today she accessorized herself with oxidized earing and bracelet. While clipping her watch to wrist Mia started talking to her son Neil.

"Neil, I have to rush for meeting urgently. Neelu is on leave. And I haven't prepare anything for dinner. What should I order for you? I will call you when I am finished meeting. Don't wait for me."

"OK mom. Can you order from Mcd, please?" Neil requested making his little cute polite face.

"Neil, how can you eat that stuff without getting bored? Just flour and cheese."

Neil made face and Mia felt very sad for him. He is such a good boy, never shows any tantrums like other children, always understanding. I need to compensate something for him.

"OK fine. But you will not repeat this for a month. Promise?

"Yeah" Neil face lit up by listening to this. Mia promptly placed the order with Mcd

"Your food is ordered and paid. I am getting late. I am leaving. Bye." Mia place a kiss on Neil cheek, take last look in mirror, rolled mauve lipstick on her lips and brushed her hair with fingers.

She picked up car keys, her bag, wore shoes and left the house. She sat in the car and put ignition key but car wouldn't start. She tried two three times but nothing. Damn what's wrong with car now? Now she has to book a cab, its peak time and cabs are not available easily. She got annoyed with the fact that she might get late for the meeting. She took out her phone and book cab on app. The cab was available in ten minutes.

'At least, this is good sign that cab is coming fast.' She dialed Jay's phone. No reply. He was in photoshoot. It must have prolonged that's why he is not picking up. She left a text mentioning about the meeting and to call her back whenever possible.

Tring tring, Mia's phone rang. It was cab driver.

"Madam, can you come to the other side of the road, otherwise I have to go ahead and take U turn to come there. It will take ten minutes more."

"No. Wait at the signal. I will come to that side." Mia Replied while thinking about delay. She didn't want to reach late for the meeting. Sooner the better. Mia started to walk across the road and bam… The tempo coming from the other side hit Mia and Mia's head crashed on the divider.

'Oh my god. The woman is hit. Please someone call ambulance?'

"Call the police standing over there."

"Anybody know who she is"

Mia heard these sentences and lost her consciousness.

#

Photoshoot finished and Jay checked his phone. Mia's text was there saying to call her as she is going to meet Tanreja. Meeting preponed. Hmm he thought, well we were prepared so that's not going to be a problem. But why four missed calls after that. Mia is aware that if I don't answer phone I call back as soon as I am free from work. What must have gone wrong? Jay was thinking fast as he dialed Mia's number

"Hello" a male voice answered from other side.

That's weird. Why Mia left her phone with someone else

"Hello. Can I speak to Mia?" Jay asked

"Sir I need to tell you something. The madam carrying this phone met with an accident and being taken to Hospital." Man answered

"What? When? Where? Which Hospital?" Jay asked impatiently

"There has been an accident on Highway an hour ago near City Mall. A tempo hit a woman. She was unconscious and is admitted in Sarvoday Hospital."

"I will be there as early as possible. But it will take me about half an hour." Jay replied while starting car. He was worried as hell, thinking what must have happened. He drove as fast as he can, to reach the hospital. Lots of questions were popping up in his mind in that half an hour.

#

Jay parked his car and ran towards the lobby of the hospital to enquire about Mia. The receptionist told him that Mia has been taken to operation theatre to perform surgery. Jay need to wait till doctor comes out from operation theatre. She asked him to wait and gave him directions to operation theatre. Jay went there and was waiting for someone who can give him answers about what is happening with Mia.

He met Mia about seven years ago. Mia was very talented and confident about her work. She was working with the agency where Jay joined as director. It was his first day as he took the charge. A new campaign was up for discussion. Mia was very quiet and not giving any inputs as the discussion was proceeding. The first thought appear to Jay that may be she is not that smart. Everyone was giving their ideas and nothing was turning up impressive. Jay asked everyone to take coffee break and rejoin again with fresh mind. He then turned to Mia and asked

"Hi, everything alright? You didn't spoke in the meeting at all. Is there any problem?"

"I am thinking on one concept, but I don't know whether it will be accepted or not." Mia replied

"That's my job to consider whether concept is good or not. You need to express it."

"I don't like imperfection. When I am confident that my concept is perfect, then only I will present." Mia replied in a strong tone.

Jay was little annoyed with the tone and was amaze to hear that answer. He further added

"If you don't share your concept thinking it will not be perfect, it will never be discussed. If it's good but have errors, we can discuss it and can make it perfect. Why don't you think that it might get accepted and share it?"

"Hmm. Still, whatever I present it has to be perfect, without any flaws" She hesitated a little. "You don't think that I am dumb and does not have anything to present? It's not like that. I will share when the time is right."

"Well. As you say." Jay shrugged his shoulders in protest. Beauty with attitude, hmm. But since it's his first day he didn't want to make any judgements about anyone. After a while Mia did come up with a brilliant concept that was just perfect. Only then Jay realized that this is someone who is smart and beautiful. That deserves the attitude he thought.

Mia wasn't blunt but she is confident, talented and yes the person who want everything to be perfect. But sometime perfection also has to face flaws and has to stand strong to get over those flaws.

#

"Who is with Ms. Mia?" Nurse asked

"I am with Mia. How is she? When can I see her?" Jay came out of memory and rushed towards nurse impatiently

"Sir. The surgery is finished. Will be shifting patient to room in some time. Doctor will like to have word with you. Please come with me." Nurse asked Jay to follow.

Jay followed nurse. Doctor Benjamin Patel arrived in his cabin and asked him to take seat. He was in his late fifties. Fair complexion, completely bald. Silver spectacles on his face made him look elegant. His narrow brown eyes with round and little chubby face gave the impression of a kind person. The gentle smile gave away assurance that he is going take care of everything. Looking at him gives feels of assurance, that he can make everything right.

"Hello. I am Dr. Benjamin Patel. I performed surgery on Mia. Who are you to her?"

"She is my fiancée and also a business partner. How is she doctor? When can I see her? Is everything Ok? Please doctor, Help me here. I am deadly worried."

"She was bought here as unconscious. Her head was injured in the accident and that must have cause the unconsciousness. Also her arm is bruised and rib fractured in impact. We performed MRI tests and are waiting for results. For now we are waiting for her to regain consciousness. The first observations of the test seems to be normal. No damage to brain. But we will confirm it only after the results."

"So you say nothing is to worry." Jay sigh in relief

"No. Nothing to worry. She will be fine. Just need to take care of fractures. And will run some more tests just to be sure. You can see her as soon as she is conscious"

"Thank you Dr."

#

Jay is sitting next to Mia holding her hand, waiting to gain her consciousness. He has never seen her like that. Helpless and still. She is a form of energy. Always doing something. Never to be seen idle. He used to tease her do you sleep calmly or in sleep also you are not still. And in reply she would say, an idle person, never achieves goals or holiday is change of type of work for achievers.... Something or other. No one should sit idle and waste time. Keep doing something was her motto. She was very independent in all ways, knows everything from fixing a tap to fixing electrical appliances. She never needs a handyman as such. She will try to fix it first, and if couldn't fix it then will ask someone to help. Helping others or solving problems was her another hobby. She believed in the quote "Help and the universe helps you in return". Now lying here still. Jay called out Mia's Name

"Mia, are you listening. Please wake up. Open your eyes and talk to me."

Jay asked Anirudha his assistant to take Neil with him as he couldn't leave Mia. Jay explained Neil to stay with Anirudha as Mia has some urgent work to finish and she is coming home late. Neil is really matured for his age. He never shows tantrums. In any given situation he will always listen and obey. When Jay told him to go with Anirudha, he didn't asked a question. I will tell him everything when Mia gains consciousness. If Neil sees Mia in this state he will be traumatized and it will be very difficult for him to get over it.

Jay spend whole night next to Mia. Next morning he got worried about why she is not waking up. If nothing is wrong what is the matter that it is taking so long for her to wake up. He asked Dr Patel about it. Dr Patel replied that Sometimes the mind and body is tired so it takes time to heal. It is better to wait for some time and see if she wakes up on her own.

"Umm" Mia whispered.

"Mia, are you feeling ok." Jay asked her cautiously.

"Yeah. My arm hurts but I am Ok. What happened? Why am I in here?" Mia asked looking at Jay with a suspicion and took away her hand Jay was holding. Jay couldn't understood what happened and why she took her hand away.

"You met with accident yesterday. And were unconscious all night. How are you now?" Dr Patel asked her while checking her pulse. He then checked her pupils with light which seems ok to him. Doctor enquired whether she had headache. She shook her head and turn towards Jay and asked "How come you are here, Jay. Where is Aamod and Neil?"

Jay got shocked on this question. Why she is asking about Aamod? And what does she mean what I am doing here. He was about to speak to her, but Dr Patel indicated him to keep quiet.

"You just gained consciousness. Your body is weak due to the accident. Take some rest. Will give you all the answers." Doctor Patel assured her and asked Jay to follow him.

"Who is Aamod and Neil?" Dr. Patel asked as soon as they reached cabin pointing him towards chair

"Aamod is Mia's Ex-husband. They have been divorced for around 4 - 5 yrs. Neil is their son. But he barely keeps any relation with them. Few times a year may be he meets Neil. That's it. I don't understand, why she is asking for him. Even she looked at me differently, this is very confusing"

"It might be the cause of post-accident trauma. She may be in shock and didn't realize. Will do some tests and see what exactly is the problem? But till them, don't force anything on her. Whatever she says agree to it, don't argue and don't ask her any questions." Dr. Patel warned Jay.

"Mia, we called Aamod. He is coming. But it will take some time. And Neil is safe with your friend. Don't worry about him. Will bring him over when you feel little better." Jay was assuring Mia. She was looking so tired, she didn't say a word and just nodded.

A few more doctors came to check Mia. Her MRI was normal, slightly showing some abnormality for which doctors wanted to confirm by asking her some more questions.

"Mia, now we are going to ask you some simple questions. Will you be able to answer those questions? Don't force yourself too much to answer. If you don't know simply say it. OK"

"OK" Mia looked a little terrified.

"So tell me what today date is?"

"Hmm..... Today is 15 June 2011" Mia replied

Neil was shocked to hear that date. It was the same day when Mia fell off from her Activa, eight years ago.

"And what do you do?" Another doctor asked her question

"I work with Smart Ad agency as visualizer"

"What is the last thing you remember doing?"

"Umm.... I was going home on my Activa. An auto came from back and brushed me. I lost my balance and fell on the road. That's what I remember."

Jay just went out of the room and started thinking. How this can happen. She just went eight years back. Last thing she remember is her last accident, and not accident happened yesterday. Is this even possible that a person can go back to the earlier memory like that. Will she ever remember this eight years? What to do now. I haven't informed Aamod about her accident. Even if I informed will he cared to come? What do I do now? Whom should I talked to?

After around half an hour doctors came out and asked Jay to follow them to cabin

"Mr. Jay, from the answers we received from Ms. Mia we think that she is suffering from amnesia. A part of her memory has been erased from her brain. Actually we don't say it's erased. It's been blocked. This accident has just blocked her memory. She remembers everything before 15 June 2011, her last accident. After that everything is blocked. Sometime it happens. When a brain suffers a same trauma, it kind of virtually reboots itself to the earlier trauma to sustain it. She may regain her memory in course of time. But at the moment we cannot tell her that she has lost her memory. She may not bear to this news and it can cause further complications."

"But how can this happen. Her MRI reports were normal. You said she didn't suffer any brain injury. Only her ribs were fractured and some bruises to her arm. How she can forget so many years. And now how we will handle that." Jay was scared and confused. He didn't understand what to do now and handle this situation.

"See. We have to help her to remember all this forgotten years. See human brain is very complicated. If we tell her now, that she has forgotten all this years and she is in 2019, it will be very difficult for her to understand it. It might destroy her memory and she will never recover it.

So it's better if we just hold up with her and let her be in 2011."

"She will asked for her husband. How will I convince her that he is not coming?"

"Can you ask him to come here and support? If you can convince him to come here, then no need to convince her."

"Hmm… This is really very difficult situation for me. I have to convince my fiancee's ex-husband to behave like her husband. No. No. How am I supposed to do that?"

"Mr. Jay, I can understand what you must have been going through. But this is the only chance we got. Otherwise we might lose hopes of bringing her memory back."

"Yeah doctor. I understand. I will do what is best for her. After all she is all I have. I will talk to Aamod and if require will beg him to do this favor for her."

Jay stood outside the room thinking about what has just happened. Not only Mia but he also has lost years of togetherness with her. He is looking through the glass towards Mia. He murmured, "Oh Mia, I feel so helpless. I want to hold your hand. Assure you that everything is going to be okay. Kiss you on your forehead to give you relief from the pain. I want to stroke your hair to make you feel safe. But I am afraid to do so because now you may get offended if I touch you. You may get angry if I kiss you. Oh Mia, I Love you so much but I am not able to express my love. I feel so deserted. I have no one than you to talk my sorrows to and now you also have forgotten me. Oh God, help me so that I can get back my Mia, the same loving, cheerful, smiling and strong headed Mia."

Jay lost in thought and someone tapped him on his shoulder. It was Anirudha.

"Neil is asking about Mia. What should I answer? Should I bring him here?"

"No Anirudha. We can't bring Neil to hospital now. Oh my god, Mia has forgotten last eight years. To her Neil is just a one year old kid. She can't see Neil. It will not be good for her. I have to ask doctor about it and then only we can decide. Can you please take care of him for couple of more days? I will visit him and will come up with something to tell him to" Jay was thinking faster than he was talking.

"No problem Jay. But we need to handle Neil also. He is very disturbed and has been very quiet since yesterday. You please come and meet him. At least he will be assured that you are there for him."

"Hmm… Will go to your house right now. As doctor asked Mia to rest for some time, and anyways for her I am just her colleague, so it's better if I see Neil."

Jay called Anvi and asked if she can come to hospital and sit for some time with Mia. Anvi is Mia's childhood friend and she has been great support for Mia through her divorce period. She was the one who supported them in their relationship. She helped them to understand their feelings towards each other and supported through the tough times.

"How you are holding up?" Anvi asked Jay after hearing the story

"I don't understand what to do now Anvi? I am too scared to face this situation. But, I have to. Will see. I am still processing the whole situation." Jay sigh and shook his head while talking.

"Don't be hard on yourself. Give some time, everything will fall in place. We will hope for best." Anvi assured Jay.

"Anvi, I have to go and see Neil. He is been asking for Mia. But right now I can't bring him here. I need to make up some story for him also. See you by lunch. If you need anything just give me a call." Jay got up and left to see Neil.

#

"Jay Uncle." Neil screamed in top of his voice to see Jay. He ran and hugged Jay tightly. Next to his mamma, Jay is the person whom he trusted and loved. Jay also loved him, cared him and whom he loved to see.

"When can I see mom, Uncle? What happened to her? Anirudha Uncle said she in hospital. Is she all right?" Neil said in low voice with tears in his eyes.

"Oh Come on. You are stronger than you look. And your mamma is fine now. Doctor Uncle asked her to rest for some time. Yesterday she fall on the road and her arm is hurt. Otherwise she is alright.

You can meet her tomorrow. Don't worry. What did you ate for your breakfast?"

"Aunty gave me bread and eggs. I also drank bournvita." Neil tone was happy again to know that his mother is alright.

"And what about your school. Did you bought your schoolbag?"

"No. Can I just don't go to school today?' Neil wanted to take the chance to skip the school

"No. Let's go home. I will pack your bag and get you ready for school. I will also come to school in evening to pick you up." Jay said firmly. At least he will be busy in school and forgot about his mother.

Neil was not happy to go to school so he folded his hand and put his head down in protest.

"If you go to school, then we might land up at ice cream parlor while coming back. What say" Jay know how to cheer him up.

"That will work" Neil cheered up with name of ice cream and started to put on his shoes.

#

After dropping Neil to school Jay took off for Hospital. Anvi was talking with Mia when he reach the room. Mia was looking fresh.

"Did you had lunch?" Jay asked Mia

"Yes. Just finished. How is Neil? When Aamod is coming?" Mia was asking about Aamod again.

"Neil is fine Mia. And Aamod is out of town for some office work. He told me he will be here as soon as possible. He will be catching the very first flight available. And he has asked me to take care of you." Anvi answered on behalf of Jay. Jay felt relieved. He wasn't prepared for this at all.

"Jay, I am hungry. Let's go to canteen and eat something. Mia I will leave now. I will visit again in the evening. Now you take rest. Visiting hours are almost over. The nurse will now shout at me." Anvi laughed and pat on Mia's hand. Mia nodded and smiled.

Jay stood there with the look what to do? Anvi tapped on his shoulder and signaled him to follow her. Jay nodded to Mia and left the room.

"How you are holding up? Oh my god, she has totally forgotten everything." Anvi exclaimed.

"I am so confused now. I have to call Aamod and need to ask for his help. We can't let Mia know that they are divorced. Doctor has specially mentioned that she cannot tolerate any more trauma. I don't know how he will respond to this." Jay's helplessness was reflecting in voice.

"Do you want me to talk to him? I can do that for you and for Mia"

"No. I will talk to him. Can you order something, I will try his cell and see if I can get in touch with him"

"Of course" Anvi started going through menu.

Jay dialed Aamod's no. It was ringing for long time. Jay thought that he will not pick up and at the same time Aamod answered the phone

"Hello, Jay...."

"Hello Aamod. Do you have a minute?"

"Hmm... is it urgent?"

"Yeah. It is. It's regarding Mia. Can we meet today? If possible now."

"Now.... What is the matter Jay? You sound stressed."

"Can you meet me Aamod? It is really very urgent."

"Ok. When and where?"

"Can you come here? I will meet you for coffee near Sana Junction."

"Ok. I will be there around 4. Is that ok"

"See you at 4."

Jay disconnected and sighed. Anvi raised her eyebrows with a questioned look.

"He is meeting over for coffee at 4. I will meet him there and explain him everything. Let's hope he agrees to co-operate" Jay was a bit relaxed now.

#

Jay reached cafe before the decided time. Apparently Aamod also came there in next ten minutes. He might have felt the tension in Jay's Voice and decided to reach early. They shook hand awkwardly. Jay place order for Cappuccinos and they settled in the corner.

"What is the matter Jay? You sounded so stressed on phone that got me worried." Aamod initiated conversation.

"Aamod there is a bad news. Mia met with an accident yesterday. A tempo hit her and she fell on the road divider while crossing the road."

"What? And why didn't you informed me yesterday?"

"She was unconscious and doctor said she will be fine by today. So I thought I will inform you today. But…" Jay hesitated for a moment

"But? Is everything alright Jay?" Aamod asked in doubted tone.

"Hmm. There is a big problem. And I don't understand how to solve it now. Do you remember Mia fell off from her Activa in 2011?" Jay was talking very slowly so that Aamod can absorbed the news.

"Yeah. But what about that now?"

"The last thing she remember is that accident. Doctor said that the trauma from accident might have block the memories and her memory almost rebooted and she is now in 2011." Jay told in one breath.

"Is it?" Aamod raised his brows lost in thoughts. He was not able to process this.

"Where is Neil? Did he knows about this accident and this memory situation" Aamod continued.

"I dropped him at school. I told him that doctor has asked Mia to rest. And I will take him to hospital in couple of days. This is not problem Aamod," Jay paused for while to give his thoughts words. He continued, "The main problem is that she is asking for you Aamod. Now she thinks that you both are still married and Neil is just one year old."

"Oh, ok." Aamod also lost in thought. "So now what. What you suggest we should do?" Aamod didn't know what he can do in this situation.

"We can't just tell her that she has forgotten all these years. Also doctor told it will be difficult for her to know that she has been divorced and that shock might erase her memory forever. So now, you need to be with her and pretend as if you both are still married. We will starts telling her the real fact step by step when we think she is ready. That might help her to process the information. Or in mean time she might get back her memory. All are ifs and buts. But initially she needs you by her side."

"Hmm. And you thought I will not co-operate. That's why you were so stressed. Come on Jay. What if we are divorced now, at one point of time I was in love with her. It was her decision to keep distance and that's the reason I kept myself away from her life. I will definitely give my support to her when needed" Jay was relieved to hear Aamod words.

"Thank you so much Aamod. I can't tell you how relieved I am." Jay expressed his relief to Aamod. More thoughts rushed in his mind. That it's not the only thing that concerns me, but there are lot of other things. Mia doesn't remember anything after 2011 and that include her relationship with me.

"Will first see doctor. He will guide us how to deal with this." Jay suggested Aamod.

They finished the coffee and headed towards the Hospital.

#

"Doctor this is Aamod, Mia's ex-husband." Jay introduced Aamod to Doctor Patel.

"Hello Mr. Aamod. Please to meet you. It's nice to see that you are here to co-operate in this situation." Doctor Patel greeted Aamod.

"My pleasure doctor. Please help me to understand how can I help?" Aamod was uncomfortable.

"See, right now Mia believes that you both are married and you just have to pretend the same."

"Hmm. But I want to ask you one question. How long do you think it will take her to recover? I mean when she will regain her memories."

"That is uncertain. But don't worry, she will recover soon." Doctor assured Aamod.

"When can we tell her that this is 2019? We have to tell her that soon as Neil is eager to see his mom." Jay was more worried about Neil now. "And Mia also asking for Neil again and again."

"Let's see how she responds after meeting Aamod. Then we can decide. It is very difficult situation you see. We don't come across such cases much often and we have to think about the patient's ability to respond as we don't want to do any more damage. Let's go and meet her"

Jay was worried how she will react. Aamod was confused as what he is going to talk to her and what if she asks questions for which he has no answers.

They arrived near the room and doctor asked them to wait outside and repeated not to show any sign of confusion and just to agree on whatever Mia speaks.

"Hello Mia. How are you feeling?" Doctor greeted Mia.

"Feeling good Doctor. Is Aamod, umm my husband is coming? Since morning I am asking, but there is no sign of him." Mia sounded angry.

"Calm down dear. He is here and waiting outside. Once I finished check-up, he will come to meet you." Doctor patted on Mia's head and checked her pulse. He gave a look at her chart and said, "Looks good. Keep progressing like this and we will send you home soon. Now I will call Aamod inside"

"Aamod, please come." Doctor Patel called for them.

"Hello. You are looking good." Aamod Greeted Mia.

"Where were you? I am in Hospital since yesterday and you are coming now. Why Aamod? I was asking for you since I regain my consciousness?"

"Sorry for that dear. I wasn't in town. I reached here catching the very first flight as soon as I got the news. If I was in town, do you think I would have come so late?" Aamod said the same excuse Jay told him to calm down Mia.

Mia and Aamod started talking and doctor asked Jay to follow him.

"Mia looks fine. I think it's time to bring Neil in. After a while with the help of Aamod I will inform her about her memory and that this is not 2011 but 2019."

"When can we tell her the rest of things like about her husband and their marriage?" Jay was eager to know.

"That she needs to remember herself. If we tell her then she might not be able to remember these years. We have to wait and watch." Doctor specifically suggested.

Jay got nervous hearing this. He was not sure for how long it will take her to remember. And he is eager to comfort her, to be with her in this situation which he was not able to. Whatever he wanted to do, now Aamod has taken his place and he is like invisible to Mia. That is killing him from inside.

He saw Anvi coming in hurry. He waved her.

"How is Mia? Did she remembered anything?" Anvi asked impatiently.

"That is not going to happen soon I think. She is with Aamod.' Jay looked disappointed and insecure.

"Don't be so insecure Jay. Everything will be alright."

Jay looked at the watch. "It almost 5.30. I have to go and pick up Neil. I promised him that I will pick him up from school. See you in evening. I will try to come as early as possible. But you know what, it's of no use, as Mia won't talk to me."

"Please, don't lose hopes Jay. Just be here. After all you are the one who is going to take care of her. I will wait for you here." Anvi patted on Jay's back and asked him to go.

Anvi waited outside for some time before entering the room and prepared herself to face Aamod. She was not in talking terms with him since the time of their divorce.

"Hi Mia. How are you feeling now?" Anvi totally ignored Aamod and Mia caught that immediately.

"I am good. Aamod is here now. So I am feeling much better." Mia smiled.

"Hi Aamod. How are you?" Anvi's tone was cold. That made Mia nervous.

"Hey what happened? Are you guys fighting or what? Is anything wrong Anvi" Mia got disturbed by Anvi's cold response.

"Oh nothing dear. She is upset because I couldn't manage to come in morning. She called me yesterday but I couldn't reach here in the morning. Anvi I am sorry for that, but I was helpless, all flights were full. I came as early as possible." Aamod signaled Anvi to behave nice in front of Mia.

"Yeah. Alright. Now you are here is more important for Mia. So I forgive you for the sake of her" Anvi pointed towards Mia and tried to ease the situation.

"You guys continue, I will bring some coffee. Mia do you want anything else." Anvi wanted to clear her mind so she chose to go out and get some air.

"Bring some muffin or sandwich for me. I want something to eat" Mia replied.

"Coffee is fine" Aamod was still uncomfortable with Anvi.

Anvi headed towards cafeteria to bring coffee and snacks leaving Aamod alone in the room with Mia.

"Is something going on between you two? Anvi's response was so cold towards you. And I just noticed that you are looking different. I cannot say exactly what, but something is different." Mia looked at him with narrowing her eyes and Aamod wasn't able to answer.

"I will go and get myself some snacks, I am also feeling hungry." Aamod made an excuse and followed Anvi without waiting for Mia's reply. Mia was surprised to his response.

Aamod went outside and decided to see Doctor Patel. As he was approaching his cabin, he saw Dr. Patel on way to visit Mia.

"Doctor, please help me. Mia is asking so many question and I can't answer her. And I am afraid, what if I answer her and something goes wrong" Aamod was looking terrified.

"I was just coming in room. Now since you are here, I think we can inform Mia the fact that she has lost some of her memory. But Aamod be careful we will not tell anything other than that. It is important for her to remember everything by herself. If we tell her anything then her brain might impose that over her memory and the real memory will be vanished. Do you understand?" doctor made it cleared to Aamod

"OK doctor as you say. Let's go"

Anvi came back with coffee, sandwich and muffin.

"Oh you bought everything. Didn't you meet Aamod? He followed you immediately." Mia asked Anvi

"I must have missed him"

"He wanted some snacks so he went immediately after you." Mia replied

"Anvi, things are feeling little weird. I don't know exactly what. But something is bothering me about Aamod. He is looking different. Am I missing something?" Anvi was shocked to hear that. What should I answer? To avoid that Anvi took a mouthful bite of sandwich and waved at Mia. Same time Aamod entered the room along with doctor and Anvi felt relieved.

"Mia there is something doctor want to tell you. Please be calm and listened to him. OK" Aamod said gently to Mia. Mia got tensed hearing this. Is something wrong with me was her first concern.

"Don't look so tensed Mia. Nothing to worry. You are alright. There is one little problem. But I am sure we will solve that too." Doctor's gentle smile assured Mia

"What you remember last is that you fell from you Activa on 15 June 2011, and you think that is the cause that you are admitted in the hospital. Am I right?"

"Yes. Where is the problem in that?" Mia looked little nervous.

"It is true that you met with an accident yesterday. But it's not with Activa. A tempo collided with you and you hit your head on road divider." Doctor said patiently. He has to unfold the truth very carefully without giving any shocks to Mia.

"Then why I can't remember it?" Mia was confused now

"Because the trauma of the accident had made some changes in your memory."

"What changes? Is really such things can happen. I mean I am not a computer." Mia said sarcastically.

"Hmm. Sometimes. But don't worry. You will remember it soon."

"And when did this accident happen, I mean the date?" Mia suspected something.

"Today's date is 8th October 2019" Doctor replied. There was total silence in the room. Mia was shocked. Her eyes widened and she bite her lip in thoughts. She felt nervous hearing the date and got just numb.

"Don't get to much nervous. This is just for some time. You will remember everything. Don't force yourself to remember. It will come easily to you like some forgotten dream. Be patient." Doctor was trying to give the minimum shock to Mia from the situation.

"What? Eight years of my life are vanished. Just like that?" Mia just don't understand how to react, what to say. She just murmured some words, "how, why I don't understand."

"Just rest for some time. Don't stress yourself." Doctor tried to calm Mia.

"Please leave me alone for some time." Mia said in low voice.

"Let her be alone for some time. Let her absorb the fact." Doctor Patel warned.

Anvi and Aamod sat in the reception waiting for Jay to come. Both of them looking relieved and tensed at the same time. Now Mia knows the fact that she don't remember eight years giving the sense of relief but at the same time the thought about when she will recover, increasing the tension.

Jay dropped Neil at Anirudha's house and rushed back to hospital. When he entered, he saw Anvi and Aamod sitting in reception area. His heart lost a beat of thinking about Mia. He hurried to them and asked, "What happened? Why are you here and not with Mia? Why you left her alone? Is she alright?"

"Calm down Jay. Just take a breadth. Mia is fine. We are here because she wants to be alone for some time." Anvi tried to calm Jay.

"Jay, doctor broke the reality of her memory state to Mia. She is in shock after hearing it and wants to be alone." Aamod patted on Jay's back.

"Hmm…" Jay lost in thoughts. At least now I can bring Neil. It is necessary for Neil to see his mom doing Ok. He is not showing but he is scared.

"Should I go and see her." Jay asked Aamod and Anvi. They were not sure but nodded.

"Hi Mia. How are you feeling?" Jay greeted Mia

"Are you aware of the news? I don't remember anything about eight years of my life. Am I still working with you? In the same agency or am I working at all? I don't know? So many questions are popping in my head. But I don t want anybody to answer it. I want to find answers on my own. I was wondering since morning that everything is feeling weird. Aamod is looking different but I couldn't make out what. You were there for me here all night and in the morning also. I saw you when I woke up. Thank you so much Jay for being with me." Mia was jumping from one topic to another. She was anxious to know everything. So many questions are making her restless. Jay was speechless at first but then he gathered himself and thought that he needed to calm her down. He need to give assurance that everything is going to be fine. She just need to give some time for it. She should not stressed herself out. He wanted to hold her, cuddle with her, stroke her hair. But he hold his thoughts and patted on her hand.

"Calm down" He took a pause and continued, "We are not working with the agency but we are running our own agency. You are very good at it and we are doing fine. See I know you have lot of questions and you want to know answers as well. But there is plenty of time for it. Just take rest and please don't stress yourself. If you stressed yourself you will feel weak. And that may cause in delay of your recovery. So listen to me and don't think much"

"Jay, you always make me feel calm and sound. You have given me support from the day you join Smart Agency. I remember the first meeting how you encouraged me and how I annoyed you with my answers." Mia smiled by remembering the scene.

"Good. Always keep smiling. That's the strength of your personality." Jay felt good of Mia remembering him.

"I am still confused about Aamod. He didn't talk much and left. Is he ok?"

"Oh yes. He is Ok. He is just scared of your accident and all this memory situation. Don't worry. I will talk to him." Jay assured.

Mia looked assured and relieved. Talking to Jay made her less stressed. She thought looking at him, that this person is so composed and steady. His presence gave me guarantee that it's going to be ok. I don't feel restless. He has some kind of magic. His voice is so magical that made me feel good. I felt that I am going to recover from this very soon. Aamod should have made me feel so but... Jay is always there for me. He understands me and if I am confused about anything, he makes it sure that I will realize it. He is always been supportive. It's my luck that I have such a person in my life as my friend.

"Thank you Jay. Thank you so much. You are very kind and supportive." Mia felt something but couldn't understand. Jay was something more than friend. But she just brushed off that thought out of her mind. He is a good friend. And I am married. My husband loves me and he is waiting outside. She reminded herself.

Jay was also thinking about Mia. She was looking weak but when she smiled, her face glowed. For the moment he thought that Mia may have felt something about him but the next moment that feeling was lost. She was silent earlier but now has become chatty as always. It made him feel alive. Mia was very chatty around him. Whenever she is upset or angry she used to become quiet and that was the clue for Jay that something must have gone wrong. Mia felt that too. She has not talked so much to anyone since morning. But now she wanted to talk to Jay. Tell him everything how she is feeling and want to know everything from him. At first she felt it weird but she started talking as it was relaxing her, feeling her good.

Jay and Mia, when they are together first thing come into their mind is sharing of thoughts, sharing of sorrows, happiness, sharing everything happened with them in the day. Jay is happy now as Mia is sharing with him as usual.

Life Back to Normal...?

It was pleasant morning. Mia opened her eyes, it was around half past six in morning. The first thought came to her mind was, where am I? For some time she stayed in bed and realized that she is at home now. Yesterday they came home from hospital. The hospital formalities took lot of time to complete and above all Doctor Patel also gave so many instructions and all of the staff bid her goodbye. That took a lot of time and by the time they reached home it was past 11. Neil was still at Anirudha's home. Today Jay will bring him back home. When she saw Neil first time after accident, she thought that he has grown up so big. What she remembered was him as just a one year old kid. And now he is eight years. So big. The idea of losing those years was painful at that time. She started crying which made Neil nervous. It was Jay who took charge of the situation. He calm her down and then took Neil to her and both hugged. That moment she never want to forget. As she was not physically much injured doctors gave discharge within a week. With confirmation of taking proper medication and rest as well.

Mia got up from bed and went to washroom. While brushing her teeth she saw herself in the mirror and realized that she has a changed a lot too. It was the first time she was looking at herself after the accident. She is looking different too. She smiled remembering how she felt when she saw Aamod after accident. Eight years makes so much changes in life. She washed her face and came out of bathroom wiping her face to towel.

"Good Morning" She greeted Aamod as he came into room.

"Good Morning. You got up so early. Wait here I will make tea. You want anything with tea. Some biscuits or something" Aamod asked her standing at the door.

Mia shook her head and went to window. She opened the window. This window was facing east. The apartment was on 21st floor which gives perfect view of the morning sky. The building was located near lake which was surrounded by a hill. So there was no obstruction of view. She looked out of the window. It was mesmerizing dawn. Orange and purple colors were scattered across the clear sky. The sky was slowly changing color from dark purple to orange with the rising sun. The darkness of night was over and it was a start of beautiful day. There was still some time for sunrise. Mia kept looking at the sky without blinking her eyes. The colors of sky, then freshness of morning, birds chirping gave her sense of liveliness. She thanked god for being alive and felt very contented.

"Mia...." Aamod called her from living room

"Can you bring tea over here? It's beautiful out here." Mia requested

Aamod came to bedroom and smiled, "You can have the same view from balcony as well! We can sit there and have our tea. Come."

Mia followed. She didn't know which room to which direction. This flat was bought a few year back which again she don't remember. She smiled and shook her head on that thought.

"How are you feeling now? Did you slept well?" Aamod asked Mia

"I am feeling good. And yeah I slept well." Mia replied.

"Jay will bring Neil home around nine" Aamod informed her

"Hmm." Mia again lost in thoughts.

It feels so different to be here. I don't know how long it will take to recover and I will remember those lost years. She was looking at the sky. The rising sun changing the orange sky brighter minute by minute. Soon this orange color will also disappear and the sky will occupy bright blue color of day. I hope one day the darkness of my memory will disappear and I can see as clear as this day. She smiled in hope. Seeing her smiling Aamod relaxed.

"Our maid Neelu usually comes by 7.30. She will make breakfast. What will you prefer?" Aamod wanted to keep conversation on.

"Anything you like. I don't have any preferences." Mia replied.

Jay has given tons of information about her regular day. Without Jay's help, it was really difficult for Aamod to manage the whole show. He was not sure whether he can do it but Jay assured that he will help and if any problem arises, he was just a phone call away. He was also worried about Aarohi. Aamod got married to Aarohi a year after their divorce. It was a not easy to convince Aarohi about the he whole situation. She wasn't ready at first, but soon she realized that it's somewhat important for Aamod also and she agreed to support him, but on conditions. Obviously she was his wife and letting your husband to stay with other woman that too his ex-wife was not easy.

#

It was her first day in college and seniors asked Mia to go and propose the boy they pointed. He was tall around 6 feet, with big shoulders and lean body. Fair skin, sharp brown eyes with such a stare that no one can forget. It was very daring act for her. She straight went to him and told him, "See this is my first day of college and as usual these seniors are ragging. These are not my intentions. I am supposed to propose you. So I am just doing what is said to be done." She kneeled down and asked him "Will you marry me?" Aamod was impressed with her boldness and he replied in his deep and authoritical voice "Why not? Let's get married." All his friends were looking at both of them. And they all laughed. But after that they shared a great amount of friendship and were always be seen together. Aamod was three years senior to her. He was very practical in nature but full of love and kindness. His last two college years and Mia's first two college years, they spend it almost together. On the day of their picnic Aamod opened up his feelings towards Mia. He was worried, what if she gets involved with someone else, after he left the college. This thought made him realize that she has become integral part of his life and he never want to lose her. Mia was very happy to realize that Aamod likes her too, as she also started liking him and wanted to commit him. Everything was perfect. Both completed their degrees. Mia completed her art school and Aamod his business school. They got well paid jobs and they got married.

Aamod and Mia were perfect couple until career mind took over.

Ding Dong. Bell rang and Aamod came out of his thoughts. That must be Neelu. He waved Mia to sit and got up to open the door

"Come on Neelu." Aamod opened the door.

Neelu was also worried to know about Mia's memory issue when Jay informed her. It was difficult for her as she didn't know anything about Aamod. She came inside and asked Mia

"Didi, do you remember me?

Mia shook her head in denial, felt ashamed to say no as she sounded very loving.

"What should I cook today for breakfast?" Neelu asked in low tone as she felt very sad knowing that Mia didn't recognize her.

"I don't know. See what's available in kitchen and prepare accordingly." Mia replied.

Neelu went inside. And started preparing. She was not aware what Aamod would prefer but she just guessed and started cooking.

Mia got freshen up and waited for Neil to come home. She was not ready to admit that she is waiting for Jay as well. Jay is handsome with warm smile and dimpled chin. His dreamy brown eyes and artist's mind made him look adorable. She has become aware of his Charming and witty personality which catches attentions of people and he will be found always surrounded by people. No doubt Neil was so attached to him she thought. Around nine o'clock Jay bought Neil home. Neil was very happy to come back to home. He was just jumping here and there and ordering Neelu for his favorites. But he did not communicated much with Aamod. Neelu was also very happy to see Neil and Jay. Mia felt it little weird that how Neelu and Neil were comfortable with Jay than with Aamod. She shook her head and thought that may be the nature of Jay, he makes everyone around him comfortable. The hour passed just like a snap and Aamod went to office. Neelu took charge of Neil and suddenly the house become quiet.

"So Mia, How are you feeling?"

"I am good. Want to start working. When can I start?" Mia was feeling uncomfortable of thought of the empty day.

"When you feel ready. It's your agency. You can start anytime." Jay smiled to know that she wants to start working.

"How about from today?"

"Today? No No. Take some rest and start Monday if you feel alright." Jay wanted her to start at the earliest. Thinking that, then he will get to spend time with her. To help her to remember.

"I must leave now. You have my number. If you want anything or you want to talk to someone, you can call me." Jay said very genuinely. Again the thought came to Mia, Aamod should have said that to me.

Everyone left for their work, school. Neelu prepared the lunch and went stating she will come around six in the evening for preparing dinner. Now Mia was all alone in the house. She first sat and tried to watch some movies on TV, but got bored immediately. She switched off the TV and went to Neil's Bedroom. She started going through his toys, his clothes. She just want something that will help her to remember. There was one photo of

Neil with Jay. She picked up that frame. It was from some beach and both of them have made sand castle and posing against that castle. Both were wearing bright sky blue beach shorts and looking very cheerful. Nothing came to her mind about that photo. She put that frame down and she stayed in that room for some time. She didn't notice any trace of Aamod in that room. Again it was wierd. She sighed and went to her room. She started going through her clothes, her cupboard. Mia smiled looking at her clothes as her taste in clothes looks the same classy as earlier. Everything around was unfamiliar. She just kept roaming around the house if anything reminds of her lost years. Her phone rang. She looked at the phone and it was Jay.

"Hi Mia. What's going on?" Hearing Jay's voice on phone Mia felt comfortable.

"Hi Jay. Nothing special. Just looking around." Mia replied

"Hmm. Did you ate lunch and had your medicine?"

"Yes. Don't worry so much. I am fine." Mia smiled

"Neil will come home around 6.30. Neelu picks him and brings him home. Then she will prepare dinner as per your choice."

"Yeah she informed me that while leaving in the morning. Jay I want to ask something."

"You don't need any permission. Just ask" Jay replied with pleasure

"How come you know everything going on here?"

Jay took pause before answering. He expected the question but not so early. She noticed. She is really very smart.

"I am always around there for you and your family. Aamod's job requires a lot of travelling and we work together so you keep updating me." Jay gave her the answer which he was prepared

"Did I bother you too much?"

"No. Not at all. We are friends for so many years and friends don't bother each other."

"Jay, What about your family? I never met anyone since accident? I want to meet your family too."

"Mia, I am not married yet. And my parents don't live in town. So I am like man with no family." Jay wanted to tell her, you and Neil are my family, you are my world. I don't care about anyone other than you and Neil. But the condition don't allow him to speak so.

"Oh… you were never in relationship with anyone until now." Mia wanted to know more and more about Jay

"No actually. I never found someone like you. So I am still single." Jay laughed.

"Hahaha. Jay don't flirt with me. I will make sure you will find someone like me."

"Oh. There is no one like you. You are single piece manufactured by God." Jay laughed loud and continued, "Just kidding. Didn't get time for this over years. I was busy building my career and thought of being in relationship never hit me." Jay was lying, he cannot tell her now that how much he is in love with her. And that she also loves him and cares for him. She will understand this soon and may get upset because he lied to her.

"Are you visiting in the evening?" Mia asked then bit her tounge thinking she shouldn't have asked this.

"Today I don't think so. But maybe tomorrow." Jay was pleased to know that Mia wants to meet him.

"Ok. See you tomorrow then. Bye for now" Mia wanted to talk to him more but was not sure about her thoughts, she preferred not to talk.

"Ok. Bye. Take care and call me anytime." Jay disconnected.

Mia dialed Anvi's no. She needed to talk to somebody about her feelings for Jay. And Anvi was her secret keeper since childhood.

"Hi." Anvi's cheerful sound made Mia relaxed.

"Hi. Are you busy?"

"No dear. What about you? What are you doing?" Anvi assured

"Can you come here? I want to talk to you in person." Mia sounded nervous.

"Yeah sure. I will come around five. Is that OK?" Anvi got worried hearing Mia's anxious voice.

"Ok. I will wait for you."

Mia was very nervous and confused. She is married to Aamod. Her marriage was not arranged. She loved him and got married. Then why she felt this connection with Jay. The way Jay treats her or the way he talk to her, makes her comfortable is what actually confusing her. She felt something while talking to him. And was worried what if, she is cheating on Aamod. Is she not loyal and having affair with Jay. The thought was making her nervous. She can disclose this with only Anvi. Anvi will not judge her. Anvi will help her out in this situation. Thinking about this Mia fall asleep.

Mia wake by the sound of doorbell. It must be Anvi. She thought and got up. She tied her hair in bun and went hurriedly to open the door. Mia opened the door and greeted Anvi hugging her. She felt comforted in Anvi's arms.

Anvi came inside and sat on sofa. Mia went inside and bought a glass of water. She smiled nervously and sat beside Anvi. Anvi drank water and turned towards Mia and asked

"Hey sweetu. How are you feeling?"

"Good. Now there is no pain or weakness as such. I might start going to work from Monday. Jay said I can join whenever I am ready." Mia was hesitated while mentioning Jay. Anvi noticed but she didn't reacted to it.

"Good for you. That way you will be busy and it might help you to recover your memory." Anvi supported her decision of going back to office.

"Shall we have some tea? I will make." Mia got up. Anvi followed her to kitchen. Mia kept water for boiling and looked towards Anvi.

"Hey, what's bothering you? You are looking uncomfortable since I am here. You can tell me." Anvi assured Mia.

Mia was not sure how to start. She couldn't find proper words to start with. She just kept looking at the boiling water. Anvi came forward added sugar and tea to boiling water and asked Mia

"Don't say you don't remember how to make tea." Anvi said sarcastically. But Mia felt terrible and tears appear in her eyes hearing those words. Anvi patted on her back and said, "Sorry, I was just kidding. Didn't mean to hurt you."

"I know. It's just I am worried about this whole situation. I don't understand how to tell you." Mia replied smiling nervously.

Mia pour tea, took one cup and gave other cup to Anvi. "Let's sit in balcony"

Both arrived in balcony and seated in chair facing the lake. It was lovely evening. Birds were chirping while returning to their nests. It feels like they were calling out their partners to come back to nests. Wind was blowing silently cooling the afternoon heat. Orange light of setting sun was filling the environment. But all these couldn't cheer Mia. She was in deep thoughts of her connection towards Jay.

"Will you speak up what's bothering you so much? I am noticing that you are so nervous since the time I am here. Now I am also getting that nervousness. Please talk to me." Anvi broke the silence.

Mia took the sip from the cup and looked towards Anvi.

"I don't know what's happening?"

"That is ok. You just survived the accident. Unfortunately you have lost some portion of your memory. It's ok for you to not understand some things. Don't be so nervous about it." Anvi was convincing her.

"You are my best friend since our school days. You know everything about me. We used to confront every secret with each other. Doesn't matter how small or how big. Right?"

"Yeah. That's true. You know everything about me and vice versa." Anvi smiled.

"Then tell me one thing, am I cheating on Aamod, did I told you anything about me and Jay. Is there anything going on between us?" Mia asked nervously.

"Why you think like that Mia. You will never do such thing." Anvi was shocked to hear.

"I don't remember what happened in all these years. But I feel too much comfortable around Jay.

I want to talk to him. When I am anxious his words helps me to relax. He was there in hospital every day and was involved with doctors about my treatment. He was even there when I woke up after accident. These all things are bothering me. Anyone can see this. This is not normal Anvi." Mia pour out everything that was bothering her.

Anvi was shocked and happy at the same time to hear this. She underestimated Mia in all this situation. Mia was really very smart and she was observing the whole time. Anvi or no one thought that Mia will notice all these things so early. At the same time she was also feeling something about Jay. The lost memory didn't affect her feelings it seems. Anvi was confused about what she is supposed to reply. Telling her truth so early was not good choice. Doctor strictly advised not to tell her anything about her past. Without telling her about her divorce how to tell her about Jay. What should I do now? Anvi just kept thinking. Mia tapped on her shoulder and asked

"Why are looking at me like this? Tell me something."

"Are you flirting with Jay?" Anvi asked naughtily avoiding her question. She thought that must be the best way to avoid this rapid question fire from Mia.

"I am asking you. Do you know anything?" Mia was little irritated with Anvi

"No. You haven't told me anything about it. Shall we ask Jay about it? Because I think he is the only person who would have known this secret." Anvi was still playing the role of naughty friend.

"Shut up. Don't do such foolishness. If it's nothing then? It will unnecessarily create uncomfort between us. You are just unbelievable." Mia said annoyingly.

"Don't think too much dear. If any thoughts are coming in your mind they must have something related to you lost memory. Just try to live your normal life. You remember doctor's advice? You have to go to your usual routine. That will help you to restore you memory. If you put pressure to your memory, it will not help. So join office and start your routine." Anvi felt guilty of not letting her friend to know the truth. Doorbell Rang. Neelu and Neil came together. And the house got noisy again.

At the dinner table Neil finished his food and went to his bedroom to finish his homework. Leaving Aamod and Mia alone on table. Aamod helped Mia to clear the table. They both finished the cleaning of kitchen and relaxed on sofa.

"How was your day?" Mia enquired Aamod

"Busy as usual. I wanted to tell you earlier. I am going to Hyderabad on Saturday."

"Hmm. When you will be back?" Mia thought he shouldn't have taken this tour since she is not yet recovered. But she didn't said anything.

"I will be back on Tuesday. There is presentation on Monday. So need go there for discussion a day prior." Aamod tried to give an explanation as he will not be here on weekend. Actually this was planned by Aarohi. So that they can spend their weekend together. She wasn't very comfortable of staying Aamod at Mia's house. And she clearly told him that he will spend weekends with her.

"I am planning to join office from Monday." Mia declared. She was clearly didn't like that Aamod is not spending weekend with her.

"Whatever you feel right." Aamod said without any concern.

There was awkward silence filled in the room. Both were unable to say a word to each other. They sat there for some time and Mia got up and said it was time for medicine. She went to bedroom took her medicine and lay down on bed to sleep.

Aamod peeped in bedroom to make sure that Mia is asleep and dialed Aarohi's number. She was restless since yesterday. She didn't said anything but Aamod felt that.

"Hi. Did you told her that you are not there on weekend" Aarohi asked eagerly.

"Yes. I am spending this weekend with you." Aamod was little nervous about this.

"Why you are sounding so low?"

"Mia just came home from hospital. I am going on tour so soon, that too not real business tour, doesn't feels right." Aamod concerned

"Hmm. So cancel the tour and stay there. I don't want to force you to spend time with me." Aarohi seems irritated.

"Don't get irritated. I am not saying I don't want to spend time with you. Mia seems to be sad about my tour. I mean, from her point of view, I am her husband and I should be taking care of her. But instead I am going away."

"Aamod you are doing favor to Jay. Mia lost her memory is not your mistake. Now you can't put your personal life on stake. Jay is there to take care of her. If you stayed there who will take care of me." Aarohi showed her insecurity.

"You are right. But for Mia's sake I feel bad. For her I am her husband and I am supposed to be taking care of her." Aamod tried to tell Aarohi his side.

"Whatever Aamod. I know this will happen, that's why I was not ready for all this act in the first place whatever you are into. I don't know till what extent this will go. I feel insecure sometimes." Aarohi cleared her mind

"Don't worry sweetheart. This is not going stretch for long. I told Jay that I will quit this if I find it impossible to continue. It's up to us. Let's give it a try for some time at least." Aamod tried to convince her.

"Ok. Let's hope this ends soon."

"See you on Saturday. Good night. And don't worry. Love you" Aamod bid bye to Aarohi.

"Good night. Love you too." Aarohi replied.

Aamod disconnected and sigh deeply. He was feeling bad for Aarohi and Mia both. Mia was his first love. Their divorce was very difficult for Mia.

But now she was happy with Jay and suddenly this whole situation has dropped landing Mia into nowhere. The once broken relationship was real to her and the one in which she was happy never existed for her. She was in complete mess. She should get her memory back. She has right to be happy again.

On the other side Aarohi was also feeling insecure. After all who will not be? Her husband was helping his ex-wife to get her memory in which she forgot that they were divorced. The situation was so dramatic that it was hard to digest. It feels like sharing your husband with someone. Aamod smiled on his situation of trapped between and switched off the lights.

#

Yesterday when Mia asked him to come over for dinner, Jay refused to go when actually he wanted to. But he promised her that he will visit today. Whenever he sees Mia, his heart aches. The whole situation has become so difficult for him, that he tried to avoid her. But that was not going to help. If he wants Mia to remember everything he has to spend time with her as usual because that will help her to remember. Sometimes he felt that Mia do have glimpses of memories but she is not expressing anything as such, so he is in dark. She is ready to join office from Monday and that was great relief for him. But he need to prepare all the staff for her arrival. He arranged a meeting for staff. Everyone was assembled in conference room as per his instructions. Jay stood up and started talking.

"Dear all, as we all know Mia met with an accident and lost a portion of her memory. She is doing good and willing to join office from Monday. As all of you were aware of my relationship with Mia, I want to ask all of you to be alert and not to say a word about it. Mia does not remember that she is divorced. She still thinks that she is married with Aamod and we all have to pretend like that. So I request all of you to please support me and Mia. I hope all of you understand." He finished and sat down on his chair.

Everyone was silent. Mia was everyone's favorite. Her helping nature and kind behavior has won everyone's heart. No one ever wanted to hurt her. Everyone was under pressure after hearing this. Anirudha, Jay and Mia's assistant got up and said, "Hey everyone. Cheer up. If Mia saw all of you with such a sad face she will be hurt. What Jay wants to say that just keep in mind that Mia thinks that she is still married to Aamod. That's it. Nothing to worry about. And maybe she will remember everything once she starts coming here. Then we can have one more reason to celebrate." Anirudha's words made everyone feel light and they started chatting and smiling.

Jay's phone rang. It was Anvi. Jay got up and went towards his cabin to take the call.

"Good Morning."

"Good Morning. So how is our hero doing?" Anvi started teasing Jay

"What hero. This hero has become zero as his heroin doesn't recognize him"

"Are you free at lunch? I have a great news for you. That will take you on cloud nine." Anvi was building a suspense.

"You can do anything for a free treat. I know you. Come at 1.30. Will have lunch together." Jay didn't left the chance to tease Anvi as well.

When it was decided that Aamod will be living with Mia in their apartment, the first thing came into Jay's mind was to prepare the house for Mia's arrival. Anvi and Jay cleared all the traces of Jay from the flat to avoid Mia's confusion. That house was bought by both of them when they decided to be with each other for the rest of their life. It was Mia's decision and choice. She loved that apartment and then turned that apartment into a happy home. Anvi helped him a lot to move all his stuff from there. It was a difficult situation for him to move out of their home, but he ensured himself that he will return home soon.

Anvi and Jay meet at the restaurant for lunch. That place was Mia's favorite place. It was cozy place with dim but sufficient lighting. The restaurant was always full but never felt crowded. Well-spaced and with light music. The dark interior of restaurant never gives out negative vibes but always felt cozy and soothing. They chose the table near window and settled. They ordered food and Jay directly asked Anvi,

"So tell me the great news for which you are asking this treat."

"Oh you will be so happy to hear it." Anvi was looking very cheerful and was very eager to tell him about her conversation with Mia.

"Yesterday Mia called me to her home. And you will not believe what she said about you."

"Will you take effort to tell me what happened?" Jay was little annoyed by Anvi's behavior

"Mia thinks that she was having an affair with you. She was asking me that whether I am aware of that. She wanted to know if she had told me. Isn't this a great news, worth a treat for?" Anvi laughed.

Jay felt the sense of hope after hearing this. His suspicion about Mia was sure that she is feeling something but enable to say.

"Great. Sometimes I also felt that in her eyes that she feels something about me. But obviously how she will confess it to me. And that made me confused how to react." Jay felt sense of joy running through his body. It gave him a hope and his face lighten up.

"We deserve a dessert for this." And he ordered an ice cream for both of them.

#

Mia was disturbed because of Aamod's tour. She wanted to catch up those eight years, wanted to talk to him, to be with him. But it seems that Aamod is not concerned about her. He just declare his going out of town. Didn't asked her whether that is OK, or how she will manage for four days. Even when she told him that she joining office, his reply was cold. It didn't occur to him to ask her whether she is feeling well. She then thought, that for me we have been married for four years but for Aamod it's been twelve years, so obviously his reaction is going to be different. And anyways Aamod was very practical person. For him his career was always comes first. Money, wealth is very important aspect for him. So bare this Mia. She explained herself.

Mia wanted to talk to Jay, but instead she dialed Anvi's number. It was ringing. She might be busy, Mia thought and disconnected. The same moment she received a call from Jay. Is that a telepathy? Mia thought as she was about to call him a while ago.

"Hello" Mia replied

"Hi. How are you feeling today?" Jay showed his concerned

"I am good. How are you?"

"Good. Today I announced to staff that you are joining from Monday. Everyone in the office was happy to hear that." Jay wanted to confirm that she is definitely joining from Monday.

"That's great. I am also eager to meet all people. Is there anyone whom I am familiar with?" Mia was worried to meet all new faces.

"You are familiar with me, don't you?" Jay asked mischievously.

"Of course, but is there anyone else. Everyone knows me but I don't remember anyone. It feels weird." Mia showed her concern.

"You met Anirudha as well. So you know him. And when you start coming to office, slowly you will get to know everyone. And it's just matter of time. You will recover soon. But for that you have to start your routine." Jay assured her

"Yes. As usual you are right." Mia face sparkled with smile.

Then they were talking for long time as good old days. After a while Mia ensured that he is visiting that day and then bid him goodbye.

#

Aamod came home around dinner time. Mia noticed that Neil is not very comfortable around Aamod. Aamod asked him about his school, his studies and Neil answered him briefly. They finished dinner and as usual Neil went to his room for homework. Mia wanted to spend time with Aamod. Aamod was sitting on sofa and watching TV. Mia sat beside him and asked him about his day. Aamod reply was cold. He was more interested in watching TV. Mia switched off the TV and hold his face in her hands. She intentionally turned his face towards him and place her lips on his cheek. Aamod turned his face.

"Aamod what's going on? Is anything bothering you?" Mia was shocked to see his response.

"Nothing. It's just some office tension." Aamod replied hastily

"Hmm. I can sense something off. You are pulling yourself away from me since my accident. Tell me what's going on?" Mia got frustrated.

"Mia, you are recovering from accident. And for some time we need to keep ourselves distant." Aamod tried to explain her.

"Aamod are we fighting on something before my accident. Is something wrong going between us? You know I don't remember anything happen in between these years. Please fill me up with the gaps." Mia tried to make her point.

"Something sort of. We have made some arrangement to clear some things between us. You may not remember, but I do. So let's just wait till you get your memory back." Aamod was giving hints to Mia

"If anything is not right between us, I would like to work that out. I don't want our relationship to go down. Now I have got chance to restart, so let's try to start over again. Don't push me away." Mia tried to convince.

"Hmm. I will think over it. Let's go to sleep. And don't overthink. Just take care of yourself. Neil is looking up to you." Aamod wrapped the subject.

"OK. But please, keep in mind to give this relationship a try. It's worth trying I suppose." Mia concluded and gave remote to Aamod

Where it started

Aamod was standing with his friends. White shirt and ice blue jeans were complimenting his fair complexion. He stood out in crowd with his broad shoulders and six feet height. That was first day of fresher's and the campus was looking colorful and cheerful. These fresher's were excited to come to college, for them the boring and disciplined school life was over and new excited colorful life of college is beginning. Some of seniors were teasing juniors by giving them some tasks as some ritual of first day, some of juniors were enjoying doing it, some were hesitant and some were shy. Aamod being the second year of degree watching all the fun happening in the campus and all his friends were expressing stories of how they were teased at their first day.

Aamod remembered his first day. He was not alone as his full clan of friends chose the same college. Still the seniors are seniors. They asked all of them to wear their shirts inside out as the ritual of first day. And then they spilt them and each one was placed in different classes with seniors. Seniors, named Vishi accompanied Aamod asked him to follow him to his classroom.

When they reached, the class was about to start. Vishi told him on the way to class that he must tell his name Mr. Prakash Awasthi when Professor asks him to introduce himself. Aamod did as he was asked and the whole class burst into laughter, the professor's name was Prakash Awasthi. Professor himself couldn't hold the laughter, and asked him to get out of the class. Vishi and Aamod become close friends after that. And for the rest of two junior years Professor Awasthi called him by name Professor Awasthi.

Suddenly he saw a girl coming towards him. She was tall and her personality was breath taking. Big, beautiful black eyes with fair complexion and nice wavy hair surrounding her face. She was wearing aqua green Punjabi suit with dupatta. That color was looking elegant on her. She was walking as if gliding on clouds and was smiling a little. Aamod fall in love with her at the first sight.

"Hi, this is my first day in college and I am here to propose you as told by seniors"

Aamod couldn't hold his laugh. She was smart and bold. She proposed him in dramatic manner and Aamod replied as why not?

It was their first meeting and Mia also felt some chemistry between them. Aamod was handsome and charming. Many other girls were hoping to make him boyfriend but no one succeeded so far. Aamod and Mia hit each other on the first day and became friends.

#

Aamod, Sam and Jeet were friends from school and Mia and Anvi were friends since childhood. Aamod always wanted Mia to be accompanied, these five were started hanging out together and soon become good friends. Mia never kept a single secret from Anvi. It was their pact to tell each other everything happening in their life. Mia did want to hang out with Aamod, and Anvi always give her company.

College started and it was time for monsoon picnic. Aamod, Sam and Jeet were planning.

"This year will not go Khandala for monsoon picnic. That's too crowded and people from everywhere come and it's nothing but chaos." Aamod wanted to go someplace where he can spend some time alone with Mia.

"Yeah, we all know. Now you don't want to go to a crowded place." Jeet teased him.

"But what I think, let's not go this year. It's crowded everywhere." Sam supported Jeet.

"Arre yaar. What nonsense? How can we missed the monsoon fun by not going to picnic?" Aamod took them seriously and both burst into laughter. Aamod got them and he just bit his lower lip in nervousness.

"You guys don't tease me. You are supposed to be helping me." Aamod put his hands on shoulders of Jeet and Sam for their support.

"Yeah. But do you think she will come for picnic with us? I mean this is not college picnic, we are going on our own." Sam was reluctant about the idea of girls accompanying them.

"For that we have to ask them." For Jeet talking to girls was a huge task.

"Leave it to me. I will ask and will make sure that they will come. See Aamod's magic." Aamod has feeling that Mia also wants to spend time with him. She will not reject the idea of picnic.

"Ok. Now that's another point of asking girls. First we need to finalize the location. Will avoid going to regular spots. Find some place which are not so famous." Aamod was very firm on going to someplace remote. They then discussed for some time and decided to go to Mahuli Fort. Since it was a trek it will not be crowded was their idea. Now the main question of asking girls. Aamod was enthusiastic at first. He was practicing the whole scene in his mind and was getting nervous as the time was passing by.

Next day when Mia and Anvi arrived, these three approached them.

After greeting each other they started chatting and apparently Mia asked

"Hey, do you guys go for monsoon picnic?"

Aamod, Sam and Jeet shocked at her question. Looking at them Anvi asked

"What happened? Why you guys looked so shocked? Did you guys were planning without us?"

"No. Actually we were not sure whether you want to come with us. We were going to ask anyway." Sam clarified.

"So where you guys are planning the monsoon picnic?" Mia questioned looking at Aamod.

Aamod was speechless. He had practiced so much to convince them for picnic and now they were asking themselves for accompanying them. He forgot what to say.

"Aamod," Mia asked again

"Oh yeah. We are planning to go to Mahuli fort for trekking. It is not far away from here and we can go by bike at the base." Aamod finally spoke.

"Oh that's great." Anvi loved the idea of trek.

The group decided to meet again after college to discuss more about trek.

It was decided that they will go by bike to the base of Mahuli fort. Aamod was excited to go on trek with Mia so much that he took all initiative of making arrangements of food, water, snacks and everything.

The day before picnic Aamod asked Sam and Jeet at their usual place. They were making sure everything they need is purchased.

"Why you took the full responsibility for picnic?" Sam was irritated by all this arrangements

"He is taking all these efforts to impress Mia, can't you see" Jeet started teasing Aamod

"Yeah. And now who is taking efforts?" Sam was still hesitant about taking girls with them

"Calm down yaar. Friend in need is friend indeed." Aamod didn't want to drop the mood of picnic.

"We need a separate party for this." Sam was still not happy.

"Ok. Everything is in place. Mia also bringing her bike. But I don't want her to drive. And I want her to ride with me. So you guys need to back me up for that. Sam you will give ride to Anvi and Jeet you will drive alone. Ok." Aamod giving non-stop instruction.

"Ok Boss. As you say. Now can we go and sleep for some time? Tomorrow we have to get up early for picnic." Jeet and Sam said dramatically.

"Hmm. Ok. We will meet here tomorrow sharp at seven. Go" Finally Aamod let them go.

They all went home. Aamod was very much enthusiastic for picnic. His mind full of thoughts of the next day. The idea of spending whole day with Mia was a dream come true for him. He couldn't sleep till late night out of the excitement. As a result, he got up late in the morning. When he reach their meeting point, all of them were waiting for him.

"At last you came. We were about to hit the road." Sam said sarcastically.

Mia was looking like a doll in her high ponytail. She was wearing grey trek pants with pink t-shirt and sport shoes. Aamod wanted to give her compliment but hesitated and kept mum.

All of them have already decided about who will ride with whom? And for Aamod's surprise Mia sat behind Jeet. He looked with anger towards both of them and started his bike.

The weather was perfect for picnic. It was romantically cloudy. It wasn't raining but drizzling. Perfect for Bike ride. As the monsoon has started a month ago, the fields were lusciously green and the air was cool and windy. Perfectly romantic day and Aamod was gloomy as Mia was not riding with him. After a while they stop for tea break. Aamod was silent and bit nervous. Everyone finished tea and snacks and was ready to start again. Anvi asked

"Hey Aamod, anything wrong? You don't look happy. What happened?"

"Nothing. I am ok." Aamod replied and everyone burst into laugh. He looked at everyone confusingly. Mia came and asked him

"Can I ride with you? I want to ride on bike and Jeet is driving my scooter."

Aamod face lit up and he immediately agreed. And again everyone started laughing. Then he realized that it was prank to tease him.

As they started their bikes Sam yelled, "We are going ahead, you two take your time."

Aamod felt embarrassed by this and started driving. Now the ride was pleasant as he dreamt of. Mia was sitting behind him. In the mirror he can see her hair were swirling around her face making her look more adorable. She started the conversation as Aamod was busy observing her beautiful face in mirror.

"Have you visited this Mahuli fort earlier?"

"No. We are also going for first time. But some of my friends did went there for trek last year."

"So, nobody knows the route to Mahuli fort?" Mia sound little doubted.

"Don't worry about the route. There are people in base village who come with and navigate the way. Just need to pay them some amount. I am in touch with them and also they are arranging lunch for us." Aamod convinced her.

"By the way, you are looking dashing in this red t-shirt." Mia complimented him and Aamod again felt that he should have complimented her first. Now he has lost the chance for that.

"What have you ordered for lunch?" Mia asked impatiently

"Chicken and bhakri. Hope you and Anvi will like it. They make very tasty chicken curry, it's their specialty."

"Great. And how long is the trek. How many hours it takes to reach to the top?" Mia's questions were never ending.

"Do you always ask so many questions?" Aamod smiled

"No. But I don't know anything about this place so I am little concern, you know." Mia gave her explanation.

"Wait and see. If I reveal everything now, you will lose excitement of visiting new place. It's beautiful, trust me, you are going to love it." Aamod comforted her.

They continued their journey and Aamod kept on telling her funny stories how Sam, Jeet and Aamod used to bunk school and how Jeet is scare to talk to girls etc. etc.

#

They reach to the base of the Mahuli Fort. There was a temple and house near the base. One person greeted them and asked them to park their bikes and pay visit to temple, in the meantime he went to arrange the guide and lunch. They entered the temple. The temple was clean and calm with no one in there. It was simple temple like any other village, just like some house in village. White and blue color painted, with some wooden pillars to support the roof. The outer walls were built only around 3 feet high. Inside was idol of Ganesha. The morning Pooja was just done and the scent of sandal incense stick, flowers decorated the idol were giving the place a sacred, holy feeling. All five of them were quiet and just soaking up in the holy feeling.

It was drizzling and the morning was a pleasant. All were craved for tea and ordered for the same. When they about to finish, their guide and lunch arrived.

"Good Morning Sir. I am Jiva, and I am taking you to the fort." Jiva introduced himself.

"Hi Jiva, This is Sam, Jeet, Mia and Anvi. I am Aamod." Aamod introduced everyone.

"Shall we start?" Jiva was all set to start.

"Yes of course. We are ready." All said together and got up.

"By what time we will reach to the top Jiva?" Mia sounded concerned.

"Madam, it depend on your speed. Some reach in 3 hours, some took 4-5 hours. But don't worry I will take care to bring you back before sunset."

They started walking the path behind Jiva. Jiva has very good knowledge of forest as well. On the way he was showing some trees, shrubs and informing about the use of it. He was also aware of the insects, birds their habits and was really aware of the forest life. In the beginning they crossed a stream. It was not very deep and with pebbles and stones. The scene was just like from some beautiful painting. The stream covered with forest, lush green beauty. Everything was mesmerizing just like fairytale story and that made Mia cheery and chatty. They wanted to spend some time at the stream but Jiva suggested to keep moving and they can stop while coming back. All have to agree as they need come back before sunset. In the starting of the trek the path was surrounded by the bushes and trees. They barely feel any rain because of trees. But as the started moving up, the trees were not as dense as the base and they were able to view the site of the valley. Half way through they decided to rest for a while. Jiva showed a nice spot. It was a huge Banyan tree and the surrounding area was cleared. A big rock was positioned below the tree, they sat there for a while. And stated looking around. Sam went around the tree and called all to look at the view. They have reached to a height from where they can see the village down. Tiny houses surround by greenery, small paths of village, the view was beautiful.

"So what do you think?" Aamod asked Mia

"Oh, this is so beautiful." Mia said in cheerful mood.

"Are you still worried?" Aamod asked her mischievously.

"Oh come on. I have never been to trek and you said neither you have ever visited. That made me worried."

"So do you trust me now?" Aamod asked her softly in ears and Mia understood what he meant by and couldn't spoke a word. She blushed by his closeness and felt a warmth in ears. She just turn to go away from there and Aamod hold her hand and pulled her towards him

"You didn't answer my question?"

"Hmm" Mia nodded and whispered with a smile on her face and tried to get away from him. Aamod let her go and smiled with satisfaction. He had a feeling that Mia likes him and now he was sure that Mia does like him.

After resting there for a while, they continued their trek. Aamod and Mia were walking behind the group. Now the path was little slippery and Mia slipped. Aamod took that chance and hold her hand.

"If you held my hand, I will never let you fall." Aamod was giving her hints and getting romantic as time is passing by.

Mia again felt the same feeling of warmth and blushed. She said nothing and just held his hand while walking through the path. For some time they were quietly walked hearing the chirping birds, smelling the rain.

"What do you think of this place now?" Aamod started the conversation.

"This is heaven. I have never been to such place. This greenery, the chirping birds, and tranquility everything is like a fairytale." Mia replied dreamily

"And in this fairytale, will you find your prince charming?" Aamod was not going to stop.

"I might find. But I have to keep looking on. Someone is following me from the beginning and so I am not able to look around." Mia replied with mischievous tone.

"Oh, so you want to look around in the forest. Then you are going to find some Adivasi prince."

"Not necessarily, some outsiders also came here like us. I can find in them also."

"So what do you think of the person who is holding your hand." Aamod asked her directly

"Hmm… well I know this person. And I think he is caring, loving, and charming. May be I should give him a chance. What do you think? Do you think he will support me in my difficult time?"

"I am sure, he will" Aamod stopped and assured Mia.

They were looking into each other eyes and just forgot where they are. Aamod came closer to Mia, now he can smell her sweet body scent, can feel her warm breadth. Mia now felt that warmth strongly but she didn't ignore his glare and keep looking at his eyes. His brown eyes were giving her assurance, his broad shoulder always ready to support, his strong arms that they will keep her guarded the whole life. She wanted to look into his eyes forever. She can smell his musk cologne, can feel his warm breath. At that moment Aamod held her face in his hand and slowly took his face near her face. Now they both can feel each other's breadth. He looked into her eyes and placed his lips on her soft lips and the rest of the world just melted away. Mia felt dissolve in that kiss. That feeling was incomparable to anything in the world. They stopped kissing and Mia bowed down her face in shyness. Aamod touched her chin and lifted her face with his finger and looked deeply into her eyes.

"Mia, I am in love with you since the day I saw you. It was love at first sight."

"I love you too Aamod." Mia rested herself in his arms and Aamod held her tightly. They didn't know how much time they spent until they heard a whistle. Mia backed away from Aamod. It was Sam. When they didn't find Mia and Aamod behind them, he ran back to look for them. He looked happy and cheery. He waved them to come and again ran away.

"Are they ok? Is Mia fine?' Anvi was worried that Mia must have hurt herself

"Yeah. Yeah. Both are ok. We have got our pair of lovebirds." Sam winked looking at Jeet.

"Where? Show me." Anvi started looking around.

"Nothing. Let's go." Sam started walking as he saw Aamod and Mia at a distance. Anvi waited till they arrive. Mia was blushing and Aamod is looking much happier. Anvi gave a questionable look to Mia, to which she shook her head and assured her of telling her later.

After a while the dense forest ended and it was all rocky path without any trees. The hill they were climbing was covered with grass. Jiva showed them the Mahuli Fort. It was still two hills away, but

Jiva assured that they will reach there in about an hour. The path they were walking was so narrow that only one person can walk through it. There was valley on the both sides of the path. That path was joining two hills. Mia and Anvi were scared to cross, even all boys were also scared a little but they didn't showed. Jiva asked them to hold a rope while crossing so they will have some support from each other. And they crossed that way.

Now they reached to toughest part of the trek. It was a big rock, and they need to climb that rock. The rock does have some hatches to climb but it was difficult for girls to make it. Anvi just denied to climb and said they can go and she will wait there. But everybody forced her to climb and finally they all climbed it through. After walking for a while on that top they finally arrived to the steps which lead them to the Mahuli fort. They raced through the steps. And reach to the Mahuli Fort.

The Fort was built by Mughals and won by Shivaji Maharaj three hundred years ago. Some structures inside fort were fallen down to form a debris. There was a temple and a stone basin with sweet water. There were some sort of caves or might be remains of palace. But nobody have taken any efforts to restore it. But still, it was magnificent. All of them were looking around and Jiva was giving information about the place.

The valley from top of the Mahuli was looking awesome. The clouds were floating below them and it was feeling like they were on clouds. The whole valley was lush green. They can see village down with tiny houses.

"This is going to be the most memorable picnic of my life." Mia exclaimed.

"Thank you guys for arranging such a beautiful spot for picnic. This is really unforgettable." Anvi added to her.

"It was pleasure to come here with you Anvi and Mia." Aamod was happy to see Mia was enjoying.

Sam and Jeet were kept smiling. All of them were hungry so they decided to finish lunch and after taking rest they will again venture the fort. They invited Jiva to join them for lunch. He hesitated at first but then agreed. The chicken curry was so tasty that they ate more than usual. After finishing meal Mia and Anvi collected all waste plates, glasses and put them in a bag to carry it down, not to make the fort area messy. Jiva surprised by their gesture and thanked them for thinking about fort. Mia just smiled.

"Mia what happened down there?" Anvi was keen to know what happened when they were lagging behind.

"We kissed" Mia whispered.

"What? Really. Tell me everything. Don't miss a small thing." Anvi was so excited to know.

"You know I slipped as the path was slippery and Aamod cought my hand. He then said if I hold his hand I will never fall. I told him that this forest feels like a fairytale. He asked whether I am looking for my prince charming. I said may be. He just pulled me towards him. We were looking at each other and then we kissed." Mia told the story to Anvi with every detail. She was blushing while narrating the story and Anvi noticed it. She started teasing her which made Mia to blush more.

On the other side the boys were teasing Aamod as Sam narrated what he saw to Jeet. And to their surprise Aamod blushed hearing it. The love story of two beautiful people has started.

After spending some more time on fort, they started climbing down the fort. The rock was a challenge to climb down. They realized climbing up was easier than climbing down.

"I was telling you guys, I will stay down, I never wanted to climb that rock. Now what, you people want me to stay on fort forever. I won't be able to come down in my life." Anvi was cursing them.

"Don't worry if you can't climb down we will just carry you." Aamod tried to calm her down.

"Carry me? Are you nuts? Is it possible to carry anyone and climb down?" Anvi was furious.

"Ok. Then we will just push you." Sam said mischievously.

"Madam don't worry. This is not as dangerous as it looks. I will help you to climb down." Jiva assured

"You are the only one whom I trust. These are not friends but they are my enemies." Anvi gave all of them a look and everyone burst into laugh.

The climbing down was really didn't felt easy. Aamod was very protective towards Mia. He was holding her hand all the way down and giving instruction every now and then.

"Aamod, we are also with you, wanted to remind you if you forgotten." Anvi said sarcastically and started laughing.

"Leave them alone Anvi. Now they don't belong with us. They have found each other." Sam didn't let the topic go.

Aamod just smiled and continued what he was doing till they reached to the stream.

"Will you able to find your way back to temple" Jiva asked

"Yeah, why?" Sam enquired

"If you want spend time in the stream, I will take your leave sir." Jiva wanted to go home

"Ok. Thank you very much Jiva for your company. We had great time here." All of them bid bye to Jiva and entered the stream to enjoy feel of water. After the whole day walking and climbing their legs were hurting. Everyone found a spot and relaxed by placing their feet in the water.

Aamod entered the water and ask Mia to join him. She didn't wanted to get wet so she shook her head. Aamod didn't listen to her and pulled her in water. At first she was little angry but after a while she started enjoying the water. The water was cold a bit but was soothing the aching body. They started splashing water on each other. They were playing in the water, enjoying. Sam and Jeet couldn't avoid joining them. Mia pulled Anvi into the water when she refused to come. After spending enough time they realized it will get dark soon. They have to return now. With little displeasure they came out of the stream, changed and started walking towards the Temple to go back home.

Everyone was so tired that they were all quiet while returning back.

"I don't want you to go." Aamod hold Mia's hand as he was not ready to let her go.

"I have to go Aamod. Don't be a baby." Mia tried to console him

"We won't be meeting for two days now. You remember we don't have college for two days." Aamod was in complaining mood.

"Hmm. Don't worry I will give you a call tomorrow and will try to meet you. Can I go now?" Mia was trying to cheer him up.

"We had such a good time today. Don't be so sad. Be happy about it." Mia continued.

"Yeah. We really had a great time today. This was most memorable day of my life." Aamod put finger on his lips and suggested her. Mia blushed again and put a slap on his shoulder.

"Now let me go. Smile and say bye."

"Mia are you staying with Aamod or coming home?" Anvi asked ironically and Mia patted on Aamod's hand and leave his hand softly bid goodnight to him.

Next day Mia called Aamod to know that he is at work. She was surprised as she was not aware that Aamod had a job. In the evening when all of them meet on their usual spot to hang out Mia wanted to ask Aamod about job but couldn't ask as all were busy looking at photos of picnic and discussing about it. She decided to ask him later.

After few days when they were sitting in canteen together, Mia opened the topic of his job. At first Aamod was hesitant about it, but then he opened up. Two years ago his father had a stroke and was paralyzed. He lost his job and to support his mother and little brother, Aamod had to accept the job offered by his father's employer. Mia was impressed to see maturity of Aamod's decision of supporting family at such a young age. He didn't want to discuss that topic and never wanted his friends to know this. Mia promised him to keep that a secret with her.

The days turned into months and months into year. The bond between Mia and Aamod was growing day by day. The final exam dates were declared and everyone started preparing for exams.

Exams were over and finally they were again happy to celebrate and discuss their future. Mia and Anvi were now in senior high school, they have to choose the stream for their degree courses. Aamod, Jeet and Sam were passing out their degree exams this year, Sam and Jeet were planning to do masters where Aamod was not sure about whether he should study further or look for a job. Mia was keen to join art school and Anvi wanted to finish her degree in computer science. The coming year was important for all of them for their future, for their career. They all agreed to hang out less and give preference to studies. Later when Aamod and Mia were alone Mia suggested Aamod to continue studies.

"Aamod I understand that you want to support you family with continuing with job. But I think you should do further studies also. Join for some correspondence course of part time studies. What do you wish to do?"

"If the situation was permissible then I always wanted to study in some business school. But that is not possible now as I just can't stop earning. And I don't think there will be any correspondence courses for MBA." Aamod told her his wishes.

"Hmm. I think there are part time courses for diploma in management. You have two years of work experience. I will enquire about such courses and let's see what we can do. Just don't lose hopes on studying further." Mia assured him. Talking with her gave Aamod a confidence to think about it. They decided to search for such course during this year so Aamod can think about it and join after his graduation.

Next year everyone was working hard. For Mia and Anvi it was a year of transition, they were about to start their next best choices for their career. Whereas for Aamod, Jeet and Sam it was career deciding year. Over all, for everyone in the group was most important year to study and that made them hanging out less. Anvi and Mia were studying together. They all meet in college and do spent some time together. Sometimes movies, sometimes just chilling at someone's house but overall everybody was serious about their studies and career.

The year passed and finally the exams were over. For Mia and Anvi, the exams were over in March but they were preparing for entrance exams so were busy studying for them. Around May everyone was freed from exams and now they wanted to go to release their stress. Suddenly Aamod's father got serious and had to admit to hospital. That made everyone tense. In few days Aamod lost his father. And everything came to halt. Everyone from the group got serious about it. Losing a father at such a young age was misery. Having a father is a firm support for a child at any age. When they went to see Aamod after few days of funeral, Aamod looked tensed and a bit depressed.

"We are very sorry for you loss Aamod. This was very shocking but you have to be courageous. You have look after your brother and mother. Now they are looking up to you." Sam tone was consoling.

"Hmm. I know. Papa was sick since he had stroke. But he was in the house. He used to guide us, sometimes scold us if we came late or something. The feeling of having someone watching over you at home is gone now. Being known that Papa is at home made me responsible to do so many things. Now who will wait for me if I am late, who will scold me if I don't eat dinner or skip lunch. He is very keen that all of us should eat dinner together. Now nothing feels right." Aamod was lost in thoughts of his father.

"Now you have to come home for your mom, your little brother Aamod. Now you are man of the house. You have to act like father towards your brother. Whatever you dad wished for both of you, now it's your responsibility to fulfil it. Just be brave and face it. Don't be depressed. It won't help your mother to face the reality. Just think of her. She lost her husband, her life partner. Now you have to be supportive for them." Mia spoke to inspire him.

"Hmm. True. I should not lose hopes, else where do they go. I should give support and must provide them what my father always wanted." Aamod realized that he needs to get out of his grief.

"You were always supportive towards your family Aamod. You are earning and supporting family since your dad's incident. Now you are decision maker for them." Anvi told him the reality.

They all gave him hug and left for home promising him of full support. It was his friends who help him to come out the sorrow of losing father and get back to normal life. The life was not as normal as earlier which will never be going to same. But Aamod tried everything his father wanted for these two brothers.

Aamod worked very hard for next two years. On weekends he joined part time diploma course and completed his management. After his diploma his employer gave him a good promotion with fat salary. His brother finished his graduation by that time and now Aamod was able to send his brother to do masters. Mia was busy with her art school. Her projects, submissions kept her busy all the time. Aamod and Mia's bond was so strong that their work didn't came in between. Whenever they have free time, they use to spend it together. Mia was so matured, she never asked Aamod for anything. Mia used to say we should be happy with whatever we have got rather than being sad for what we don't have. Days passed in months, months passed in years. Aamod brother graduated from business school with a placement in Dubai. Everyone was happy to see the success of his brother. Aamod took this as his own success and threw a party.

Mia completed her degree and joined as junior visualizer an advertising agency in suburbs. Everyone was settle in their profession.

The Beginning

Mia loved her job. She was talented enough to make a notice of her efforts. In just a year she proved herself and was appraised by her bosses. Remarkably talented with lovely personality she became everyone's favorite. Aamod also settled in his profession and being a true career oriented and workaholic he become a person without whom team felt incomplete. Aamod and Mia both were in different profession but always respect each other. They meet whenever they find time. Aamod's mother was aware of his feeling for long time. She even asked him few times about his future plans regarding Mia and every time Aamod just knock off the topic saying when the time is right.

Now Mia's parents were also aware of the fact that these two are more than friends. They were asking Mia as well for her wedding plans. Mia used to keep quiet about it. She was waiting for Aamod to ask her, she didn't want to force marriage on him.

Mia's mom asked Anvi about it as Mia was not responding to them.

"Anvi, did Mia talk to you about her wedding plans?"

"No aunty. Why? What happened?" Anvi stumbled to answer

"I and her dad both asked her about it. But she never responds. We are aware about her relationship with Aamod. But what about marriage?" Mia's mother showed concern

"Aunty I will try to speak to her regarding this. Don't worry." Anvi didn't know what to say.

That same day Anvi called Mia. They decided to meet on Friday for dinner. Mia and Anvi have decided to dine at least once a month together to catch up with each other since both of them got busy with their profession. Their friendship was so nourished that even they don't meet for days, it didn't show up when they meet. They get along as if they were meeting every day. That's the sweetness of their friendship. The compassion and love was same on both the sides.

On Friday Anvi picked up Mia from her home. Both decided to go to a terrace garden restaurant to have dinner. They wanted some quiet place to go, so that they can talk to each other, share everything with each other. The restaurant was bit crowded as it was Friday but they found a quiet corner which was made for only two people, next to an artificial waterfall. The sound of water and Kenny G's music softly playing in the background made the evening blissful. After settling down Anvi directly asked Mia about her relationship and its seriousness.

"Why you are asking me this now. Of course I am serious about our relationship." Mia replied immediately.

"Then why you are not disclosing it with your parents?"

"Did mom talk to you about it?" Mia sounded curious.

"Aunty called me the other day to ask about your plans for wedding."

'Hmm. Mom and dad asked me also couple of times. But what should I say. Aamod never talk to me about marriage or getting married. And I don't want to force him for wedding. He must ask it from his heart. How can I ask him?" Mia was little nervous about the topic.

"Yeah. You are right. But now you both are together for so many years. You both love each other since college days. It's been six to seven years now. And now you both have good jobs, great careers. Your parents think now it's time to think about marriage. And they are also not wrong in a way. All your cousins and friends are getting married."

"I know. I also want to marry Aamod. But he is not asking. What should I do?"

"If you can't ask him, I will ask him?" Anvi said cheerfully.

"What you want to ask him? Whether he will marry you?" Mia started laughing uncontrollably.

"Shut up your nonsense. If you wish to marry, I think you should ask or at least give him some hints." Anvi trying to convince Mia. The food came and they continue the conversation while having starters.

"What hints should I give? I don't understand." Mia was not sure about opening this topic with Aamod.

"Wow. This place serves amazing Chinese food. I just love this lemon chicken." Anvi was indulging the food.

"I am asking you about hints. Is this what you want me to say to Aamod? Then we are wedded." Mia controlled her anger.

"I was just enjoying my food. You think about your marriage and your hints. Let me first enjoy the food." Now its Anvi's turn to laugh. Mia slapped on Anvi's hand and looked at her irritatingly taking her plate in hands she said

"Anvi, you bought this topic up and now you want to enjoy your food. Just finish what you have started. You are such a foodie. I will not give you the plate till you find answers." Mia gave ultimatum.

"Ok. Ok. Give me my plate, will discuss this while eating. You were asking about hints? Right?"

"Hmm" Mia was still angry.

"You tell him that someone has bought marriage proposed for you. Then he will feel insecure and may ask you." Anvi said thoughtfully.

"I can say my parents asking me to get married."

"Hmm. That will also work. Ok you will say him this and let's see what action he takes. Now can we order some main course please? I am very hungry." Anvi said dramatically making her face.

Mia and Anvi returned home with practicing and mimicking that how Aamod will react hearing about the proposal.

#

Aamod and Mia don't miss meeting on Sundays. This time Aamod insisted on meeting over dinner. He told her he will pick her up at seven sharp. Mia wore her favorite pastel pink color t-shirt paired with her dark blue jeans. To accessories she chose to wear white stoned long earing and matching bracelet with it. As she was tall, she never wore footwear with high heels. She chose to wear her beige pumps to match with her attire. She completed her look with light layer of compact and a dash of pink lipstick. While looking at herself in mirror she blushed after thinking about Aamod's reaction.

When Mia arrived to their meeting spot, Aamod was there and was early waiting for her. He was looking killing handsome in his all-time favorite white shirt and ice blue jeans.

"Hi Handsome. This combination gives you a killing look." Mia greeted him with broad smile.

"Why you are so beautiful? Every time I see you, I fall in love with you again and again." Aamod kept looking at her with dreamy eyes and Mia blushed and bite her lower lip.

"How can you feel shy after so many years with me? I love it." Aamod laughed and Mia slapped him on his arm.

"Will you keep talking here or shall we start moving?" Mia said with fake exasperation.

They reached to restaurant which was located on a hill from where one can get the lovely view of city. In the evening the city lights look like twinkling stars from the hill. The restaurant was situated on lawn. Tables were arranged in such a manner that no one will have any interference from other guests. The bushes were lit by placing strings of lights all over it, every table was decorated with a candle and a rose. The melodious tunes of Yanni's piano were frolicking softly in the background. The ambiance created at the restaurant was purely romantic. Aamod chose the table which has a better view of city. Mia was impressed with the Aamod's choice of restaurant. She was anxious to ask Aamod about his idea of marriage. But she decided to push that aside as she didn't want to ruin the evening, the romance, the view.

"How is the view sweetheart?" after settling in the chair Aamod asked Mia.

"Oh it's beautiful. I wasn't aware that our city does have such a fancy and romantic restaurant."

"You have a lot to discover dear." Aamod mischievously smiled.

"How did you got to know about this place?" Mia asked Aamod with a smile on her face

"I always keep looking for new places."

"Hmm. Like Mahuli fort."

Both laughed on the memories of Mahuli. Apparently after Mahuli they went to lot of places for picnic but Mahuli was their special place. That day was unforgettable for not only for both of them but also for the whole group.

Aamod held Mia's hands and kissed softly. Mia blushed by his action. Though it was his usual action, every time Mia used to blush.

"You are very beautiful Mia. Do you know that?" Aamod gently pushed the strand of the hair running down her cheek, with his finger behind her ear

"Beauty lies behind the eyes of the beholder. You love me, so I am beautiful for your sight." Mia said modestly.

"That may be true. But I just can't get my eyes off you when you are with me."

"Now please shift your focus to the menu otherwise we will be starving for the whole time." Mia tried to change the topic.

"You are such unromantic. Your boyfriend is complimenting you and all you can think about is food. Such a shameless girl." Aamod said in fake irritation.

"Yeah. Love doesn't fill your hungry stomach mister." Mia and Aamod both laughed and started looking at menu. They ordered some cocktails and starters.

"What's going on with your new project?" Mia asked Aamod.

"Oh don't ask. Everything a chaos right now. Client has approved the budget and wants to start the project by end of this quarter. Many things needs to be lined up and a lot to prepare. I hope this goes all well. This is a big project for my team as well for the company. If we succeeded to complete within time then I am definitely up for the promotion. This projects has to be completed successfully in time. Lot of pressure for me and my team."

"Oh don't worry when Mr. Aamod is handling the project, no one dares to mess it up. I know you will work very hard and achieve success as usual." Mia said while taking sip of her cocktail. She was very confident about Aamod style of working and execution of his projects.

"Hmm. Hope so. And tell me, what about you? Any new clients, or any new pitch?"

"Umm. This time our team has been chosen for the designing a campaign for the new pitch. Lot of arguments and brain storming is going on. But we haven't reach to anything so far. In this week we have to finalize the topics and start working on it as the presentation is due. Lot is going on."

From there onwards they were discussing things about their work, the movies and lot of other things. Mia decided to ask about the marriage some time later as Aamod was very tense regarding his project.

They headed for home. It was full moon night. Moon was shining brightly in the sky making the night perfectly romantic. Mia was in pleasant mood as the evening has passed as per her expectation. They started climbing down on bike. The road to the restaurant was covered with trees. Mild wind was blowing. Somewhat sweet, some earthy scent of night was floating through the wind. Around a corner one can have the best view of the city from a top of hill. It was a big turn and for that a lot of area was cleared. Aamod slowed down the bike and asked Mia if they can stop there for a while to look at the view. Mia agreed. Aamod parked the bike and they stood there facing the view.

"Wow, what a beautiful view. The city looks like a paradise from here.' Mia said contemplating the view.

"The city which is crowded, polluted looks like paradise if viewed from a distance. Isn't it?" Aamod was little philosophical.

"Hmm." Mia rested her head on Aamod's Shoulder. She wanted to gather the image of the city in her memory. She wanted to gather all these beautiful moments and store them forever.

"Mia, I want to ask you something?" Aamod hold Mia's hand and asked tuning his face towards her.

"Since when you need permission from me?" Mia said looking into his eyes with a smile

"I don't know how to ask? It is something very important and for long time I wanted to ask you this. But I don't know whether you are ready for this?" Aamod sounded nervous and eager at the same time.

"Now don't give me tension about what you are going to ask? Have I ever refused to you on anything?" Mia didn't have a clue what's in his mind.

"Mia," Aamod took a big pause, Mia was listening with all her attention.

"We are together for almost six years now. Don't you think we have to go a step ahead in our relationship?" Mia was surprised to hear this as Aamod was asking the same thing which she wanted to ask. Did he read my mind? She again felt a strong bond or connection between them. They always communicated their thoughts without saying it a loud.

"I am listening Aamod"

"I love you Mia and I want to spend rest of my life with you. I want us to get married. Will you marry me?" He hold her face in his hand and looked in her eyes and spoke in one breadth.

"Yes. Of course, I do want to spend rest of my life with you." Mia smiled with joy.

Aamod felt so relieved and his face lit up with contentment. Mia was on cloud nine. Her eyes filled with tears of joy. Aamod face changed from a happy to tense,

"What happened Mia? Why your eyes filled with tears? Did I said something that hurt you?"

"No. These are tears of joy. I am so happy, I can't express it. Everything feels like a dream come true." Mia said with smile on her lips.

"I can't see tears in your eyes." Aamod wiped the tears with his lips and kiss her eyes.

He gently place his lips on her both cheeks. Mia felt his warn breadth. His masculine fragrance filled her with joy. He gently set aside her hair behind her ears and started looking into her eyes. Mia felt assurance for life in those eyes. She wanted to forget everything looking into those brown eyes. Mia moved her lips towards his ears and whispered I Love You. That was the moment, Aamod took charge and place his lips on her soft lips. The kiss was giving promise for life to each other. It was a vow to keep each other happy and to support each other in crisis. It was consent of their love, passion and intimacy. They stopped kissing and look into each other eyes and silently promising to be together forever. He pulled her towards him and hold her tight against his chest. Mia rested her head on his broad chest in peace. They were embracing each other and don't want lose the moment, the night and each other.

"I will ask my mother to meet your parents for further discussions." Aamod said while cuddling her hair and placed a kiss on her forehead. In that moment Mia thought she is luckiest person on the earth.

The meeting between Aamod's mother and Mia's parents happened soon after that. Mia was single child, being pampered always but never spoilt. On the other hand Aamod lost his father few years ago, so all the responsibility of marriage was going to be on his shoulders. Aamod and Mia wanted a small gathering for the marriage only close friends and relatives. All the parents were very happy to set the wedding date and all the other arrangements. They set the wedding date in December. They were against the big fancy weddings. Everything went smoothly and the December arrived.

Anvi, Sam, Jeet were very happy to see their best friends getting married. On the day of wedding Anvi didn't left side of Mia for a moment. Mia was looking like princess in the mauve saree she chose for wedding ceremony. Her grandmother's pearl choker, and gold necklace were looking beautiful with that saree. Gold and green bangles were enhancing the beauty of mehndi on her hands. With mehndi on foot, anklets on ankles, waistband on her waist, armlet on her arm and eardrops on ears and nose ring making her look like a queen. She was the most beautiful and happiest bride. Aamod wore off white silk kurta with Magenta stroll. Both of them were looking like a fairytale prince and princess. Mia was the most smiling bride anyone has looked so far. With selected guests and friends the wedding ceremony was completed very pleasantly. Everyone on that room was happy than ever be.

After biding goodbye to all guests, Sam, Anvi and Jeet drive them to hotel. They insisted Aamod to carry Mia to the hotel room. Mia was feeling very shy, but no one listened and Aamod picked her up in his arms and started walking though the corridor. Everyone present in the lobby was clapping to encourage the couple. Aamod whispered in Mia's ears, "I am going to recover this efforts madam, you look forwards to it." Listening to this Mia pinched him.

All of them entered the room. Anvi, Jeet and Sam decorated the honeymoon suit for the couple with rose petals and scented candles. Soft music from their favorite Yanni was playing. The ambience was extremely romantic. Aamod put Mia down and turn to say bye to them. But they all made themselves comfortable on the sofa and chair. They started eating fruits lied on the table and were just chatting. Aamod was surprised to see why they were not leaving. He signed Jeet what's going on. But Jeet paid no attention to him and kept eating grapes from the fruit bowl.

"Ok guys. See you tomorrow." Aamod finally said to move them away.

"What? Where are you going?" Anvi burst into laugh.

"You are not supposed to go anywhere Aamod, it's your night." Sam said mischievously.

"I am not going. You all need to go now." Aamod whispered giving glance at Mia.

"What are you whispering? We can't hear." Sam said loudly.

"Shh…" Aamod face was showing irritation and all of them started laughing.

"We will go, but for that you have to pay some taxes by completing some tasks." Anvi finally said a word about going.

"Shoot. I have to complete task to shoo you guys away." Aamod finally felt defeated by his friends.

"Mia, come here." Jeet called Mia and asked her sit on the sofa. He then pointed Aamod to sit beside her. They looked at each other and sat in sofa with questions on their face.

"Hmm. So newly wedded couple, we want to know how you will survive this marriage. So we have come up with some tasks that will gives an indication of your married life." Sam started talking.

"Now don't start lecture. Just tell us what we have to do?" Aamod was impatient.

"Calm down my dear friend. Have patience. Now I will give you first task. You know each other for a very long time. So we want you to describe your partner in a song. And if we find it OK, then will move to next task, or you have to sing another song. Aamod your turn" Jeet described first task.

Aamod waited for a moment thinking of a song. And suddenly he remember the song from Modern Talking

"Deep in my heart there's a fire, a burning heart

Deep in my heart there's desire for a start

I'm dying in emotion, its my world in fantasy

I'm living in my, living in my dreams

You're my heart, you're my soul

I'll keep it shining everywhere I go

You're my heart, you're my soul

I'll be holding you forever Stay with you"

Mia started clapping with tears filled in her eyes. She felt so special and loved.

"Wow…. That one was great. Aamod you sing horrible but I can feel the love between those lines. So, I will pass you. Now Mia it's your turn." Anvi was damn pleased by the song Aamod Chose.

Mia was stunned. Which song to sing for Aamod? She had no clue. She kept on thinking and thinking.

I have a dream, a song to sing. To help me cope with anything

If you see the wonder of a fairy tale. You can take the future even if you fail

I believe in angels. Something good in everything I see

I believe in angels. When I know the time is right for me

I'll cross the stream, I have a dream

I have a dream, a fantasy. To help me through reality

And my destination makes it worth the while

Pushing through the darkness still another mile

I believe in angels. Something good in everything I see

I believe in angels. When I know the time is right for me

I'll cross the stream, I have a dream

Aamod smiled and put his arm around Mia's shoulder in affection and pulled her closer.

"Wow…. You two are really made for each other. But in this task Aamod you won. Now will move to next task. This is just like dumb sheraz, but instead of movies we will give you a message which the other one of you need to descript. Mia this time you play first. Here is the message." Anvi handed a chit to Mia. Mia read the chit and give an irritated look to Anvi. Anvi laughed as the chit said, if you bring potatoes, I will give you a kiss.

Mia kept thinking about how to narrate this to Aamod. She started making hand gesture which was hilarious to see. But after a while Aamod understood her gestures and finally said that. It was Aamod turn then, his chit said 'if you gave me kiss, I will take you to dinner.' Again same thing happened Aamod made some gestures and Mia understood it. Anvi, Sam and Jeet together said "It looks like you both are connected mentally." And all laughed.

Aamod thought it must have been over by now, but no. Jeet bought a glass of milk from somewhere and now they need to drink that milk sip by sip. One sip by Aamod and one by Mia. Now both of them were in playful mood. Aamod took one small sip and winked eye looking at Mia. By this gesture of Aamod, Mia blushed and took one sip. But afterwards she also winked at him and both smiled. Then come the most crucial task for that night. Sam had bought and Magai Masala Pan. Now Mia has to keep half of the paan in her mouth and Aamod would eat the other half of it. Listening to this Aamod sarcastically said,

"You all are getting married someday, and I will see to it that you all will repay in double."

"Ok, Okay we will see. Right now focus on Mia and that pann." Sam patted on his back and laughed.

They both have became so much playful by that time that they didn't hesitate a bit doing this task. And Aamod threw his fist as a winning gesture.

"Anything else you want us to do. Come on we are ready to play anything" Aamod was completely in joyful mood.

"Let's play antakshari" Jeet glanced at Sam and suggested. They just want to tease Mia and Aamod by spending time in their room.

"Go to hell and play there." Aamod said slapping on his back and everyone laughed loudly.

"If you are done with this game nonsense, get your butt out of this room." Aamod almost pushed them.

"Oho. Now you got married, we are like obstacles in your way. We are you best friends how can you ask us you get out. How dare you?" Sam said dramatically.

"Yeah yeah. You all are my best friend who are trying to waste our most important night this way. Get out." Aamod started pushing them.

"Mia, at least you let us stay here for some time. We want to spend time here. We haven't hung out like this in months. You both made us all so busy in your wedding preparation, now let us chill out for some time." Anvi said mischievously. Mia looked at Aamod. Aamod shook her head signing don't fall for their plan.

"Hmm. Actually you are right. But now I am married to Aamod and I have to follow what my husband says." Mia said making dramatic face.

"You too Mia." Anvi exclaimed dramatically shaking her head.

All laughed loud and Sam, Anvi and Jeet left the room.

Now Aamod and Mia were alone in the room. The games they played before made the air thin in between them and they were in joyful mood. Aamod went to music player and changed the music to one of Kenny G.'s romantic track. He then approached Mia and extended his hand for dance. Mia smiled and held his hand. They both started dancing slowly on that musical notes. Butterflies started flying in Mia's stomach with Aamod's romantic touch. Mia deeply smelled the masculine scent of Aamod and rested her head on his chest with eyes closed. Aamod lowered his head and rubbed his nose behind her ears. That sweet intoxicating aroma of her took him to the highest peak of love. They both were in that dreamy state for some time feeling each other and complete. Aamod opened his eyes and looked at Mia, she was resting her head on his chest and her eyes were closed. He held her face in his hands and looked into her eyes. She also responded with looking in his eyes. And at the same time both said "I am in Love with you." It was so perfectly matched timing that they both smiled and Mia hugged Aamod tightly. Aamod pulled her apart and started kissing her softly on her forehead, eyes, and cheeks and then he placed his lips on her soft lips. Mia just melted down by that kiss and responded him the same way. Both of them flowed in the ocean of love and romance. Their two bodies blended into one and they were on cloud nine. They were at the pinnacle of happiness.

Difficult Times

The newly married couple chose Mount Abu for their honeymoon. They spend a week in Mount Abu. Those eight days were magical for Mia. Aamod was with her all the time. No work pressure, no phone calls, nothing but only the two of them enjoying each other's company. Aamod was taking so much care of Mia that it made her feel like a princess. Every wish, every demand made by Mia was last word for Aamod. They enjoyed the shikara ride in Nakki Lake. The myth was a saint dug down that lake with his nails so the lake was called Nakki Lake. They visited the Brahmakumari Shantivan and the beautiful rose garden opposite that. They visited the beautiful Dilwara temple which was treat to Mia. The finest architecture and sculptures in that temple were so mesmerizing that left Mia speechless. The artist in her was inspired by that beauty of art. After spending those heavenly eight days in Mount Abu the newly wedded couple returned to the real life of the city with a heavy heart.

The routine started. Aamod's mother accompanied them for few weeks after marriage. After a while she decided to move to Dubai to stay with

Shekhar, Aamod's brother. He was alone there and asked her to come.

#

Alarm rang, Mia switched off the alarm and look to her side. Aamod was still in deep sleep. Getting up in the morning to see your loved one on your side is a blissful sight. After opening eyes, getting into each other's arms and kissing good morning was like a ritual for both of them. Whoever gets up first would hug the other person and wake him or her up. Mia took Aamod's hand under her head, hugged him and wished him good morning.

"Hey sleepyhead, Good morning."

"Good Morning sweetheart." Aamod wished her and hugged her tight while placing a kiss on her lips. Mia cuddled for some time and then freed herself from embrace to get up.

"Hey, stay for a while. Don't get up so soon." Aamod said while pulling her close to him.

"You take ten minutes nap. I will wake you up once the tea is ready." Mia freed herself and got up. She tied her hair into a bun and went to freshen up.

First few days were magical. Living together, getting to know each other habits, likings was romantic. Days turned into months and months to a year. On their first anniversary Aamod gave Mia a great surprise by gifting her a diamond ring. Aamod asked Mia to meet him near jewelry showroom. She was surprised to hear that but then Aamod told her that let's go for window shopping. Let's be pretend to be rich for a day. She was thrilled of the idea and went along with him. The salesman was showing different rings and Mia was trying all of them but none of them made her feel this is the one. At last she saw one ring and just fall in love with that ring. She whispered in Aamod ear that whenever they will be able to buy, they will buy that kind of ring. Aamod smiled and asked her to try some more. In mean time he will also look for something and left her there. After a while salesman came to her with the bag and offered her the bag. Mia confused and told salesman

"You must be mistaken. This doesn't belong to me. I didn't purchased it yet. We are still looking."

"No mam, this is yours. Sir just bought this." Salesman said with a smile.

"Aamod….. Oh my god. Did you…. Wow really…." Mia was speechless and couldn't find words to express her pleasure. Aamod came near to her and wish her

"Happy first anniversary sweetheart"

"Happy Anniversary dear. I am so happy and so lucky to have you as a husband." Mia couldn't believe that she just owned a diamond ring. Wearing a diamond is every girl's ultimate dream. She was as speechless as a one can be. She opened the box and offered her hand to Aamod and requested him to put ring on her finger.

While coming back she called Anvi. When she informed her about the diamond ring, both kept yelling on phone. Mia was yet to process the fact about the diamond ring. She was looking at her finger all the time and smiling all the time. Aamod was happy to see her happy.

After a month of their anniversary, Aamod took Mia to a seafood festival. The festival was hosted on huge ground next to beach. At the entrance two mermaids were placed to greet the guests. The whole decoration was based on the theme of ocean colors. Sea green, turquoise, blue shades were used all over the place. Mia was thrilled after looking at the decoration of the event. Shacks were made of coconut leaves, some stall owners also hanged the hammock to attract people. It was beautiful pleasant day of January. Sky was clear and weather was pleasant. Mia and Aamod had planned to spend the whole day at the festival. The folk dancers and musicians were performing at the festival to entertain the people. Aamod and Mia started their day with fish food varieties and ended the day with the fish food.

Next day Mia woke up with nausea and thought that too much of seafood must have made her sick. She took some medicines for it and went to office. When for the next two days she had nausea in the morning, Aamod forced her to go to see doctor. After a routine checkup doctor congratulated both of them for expecting a new member in their life. Mia was pregnant and that was the reason for her nausea. Aamod got tensed as he thought he is not yet ready for becoming parent but Mia was very excited to hear the news. It was the difference between thinking of male and female. The responsibility, the arrangements, the funding is usually taken care of a male partner whereas the female is looking towards the love, affection and care of the child. As Mia was super happy, instead of showing the stress about being a parent and other responsibilities Aamod chose to follow the path of happiness with her.

On realization of Mia might not able to continue working post-delivery, income will decrease and expenses will increase, Aamod started thinking about how to make more money. He was aware that if he got promoted, his salary would definitely increase, so he started working towards it. That meant more office hours and more responsibilities. On the other side Mia was busy nesting the house for her beloved baby. She wanted everything perfect for the little one.

Mia gave birth to a healthy and beautiful baby boy. They both named him Neil. Aamod was on cloud nine when he saw his baby boy. A woman becomes mother when she hears the news of her pregnancy but a male becomes father when he holds his child in his arms. The moment when Aamod took Neil in his arms, he felt that how much this little baby meant to him. How he is depended on him. His heart felt with affection and love and care for his little boy. Neil was Mia's life. After delivery she took a long leave form her office and was totally dedicated herself to take care of Neil.

A year passed. And now it was time for Mia to join office. She joined the office with heavy heart as she left Neil with her mom. They decided that for first few moths her mom will take of Neil with the help of a babysitter or maid. Once the Neil is used to babysitter, he will stay at their home.

The life in the city has so much speed that no one has time to breath. Every morning is like a rush hour. Getting ready for office while making lunch, breakfast was surely a difficult chore to Mia. Aamod was of no use in morning for any housework. He used to get up, get ready and rush for the office. He was of no use to take care of Neil as well. Mia was the one who is responsible for everything related to Neil. Lunch and breakfast ready or not, he used to leave for office at his time. He never force Mia for his meals but never helped her either. Before marriage as Aamod was always busy with his work so never helped at home. He never touched any house chores. But that was in Mia's case also. She liked to cook or clean but before marriage that was her choice and now it was her responsibility. Which made her nervous. Making different dishes on weekend or cleaning the kitchen after dinner was her contribution in house earlier but now it got included in her daily routine. Getting up early, making breakfast, tea, lunch, and then getting ready for office was making her run every minute. Mia was very keen about doing things perfectly. She has habit of doing every job flawlessly. Before leaving house she wants her house neat and tidy. She was always in hurry, always late to leave for office and always in stress to reach office in time. As this was also a practice not to get late. The routine is making Mia nervous and traumatic each and every day. She started becoming angry all the time for not being perfect in all her chores. She wanted to do everything and was not able to finish all her chores on time. Doing everything started making her always exhausted and that made her more and more irritated. Because of this her relationship with Aamod started getting affected. She started cribbing all the time that Aamod don't help her or don't come home early or something or the other. Aamod was not able to understand what's wrong with Mia. The chirpy, cheery, talkative Mia has now become angry, annoyed and always irritated. She was not the same girl he fall in love with. He wanted to understand her problems but he was unable to understand the root cause of her behavior. For last couple of years Mia was so busy in her schedule of Neil and office that she was never available for Aamod. Whenever Aamod needed her as a companion or as wife or as a friend, Mia always has something or the other things in mind, and she couldn't focus on him. That started making Aamod drifted away from her. He started spending more time in the office. The same time he met Aarohi. Aarohi was working in one of client's office. At first they were just talking business on phone, but at one of the business parties they came face to face and became friends. Earlier business talks now turned into frequents chats and soon they meet for dinner on regular basis. Mia was so busy that she never noticed the change in Aamod's behavior and took everything for granted. At first she didn't mind Aamod coming home late, but when it became regular Mia got irritated and started asking questions.

Valentine's Day was coming. For last couple of years Mia couldn't go out with Aamod as Neil needed her. But now since Neil has habit of staying without her, she decided to celebrate Valentin's day this year. She requested her mom to take care of Neil for that evening. A day before she asked Aamod

"Hey, have you made any plan this year to celebrate Valentine's Day?"

"Nothing. Are we celebrating?" Aamod was completely clueless

"We can. I asked my mom to take care of Neil for evening. We can go out for dinner or may be for long drive." Mia showed her excitement to spend time with Aamod. But Aamod didn't show any enthusiasm which made Mia felt ignored. Still she asked him again.

"Let's go somewhere. For so long time we haven't spent time together. I need this."

"Mia, you are well aware that I am so busy. I don't have time on weekdays. And this is too eleventh hour decision. I cannot reschedule my tomorrow. I have lots of things to do." Aamod showed his inability.

"Aamod I am not asking you to take leave. I am just asking you to come home early, so we can go for dinner. I know I am asking at last moment, but can't you try to come a little early. Or if you want I will come to your office and will go. In this way you will save time of reaching home."

"Mia, I am sorry. But tomorrow is really not possible. Will go for dinner on Saturday." Aamod didn't like the option of Mia coming to his office.

"I really don't know how long it will take me to finish my work in office and I don't want you to come there and wait. I will feel uncomfortable then."

"Hmm…. It seems you don't want to spend time with me. I was so looking towards this evening." Mia felt very sad as she was dreaming about some romantic time.

"Mia, don't be so dramatic. You were always busy with Neil or housework. Now you planned something without asking me. How do you want me to react? Do you want me to run to you throwing my work away? But sorry this will not happen. Next time whenever you want to plan anything include me at very first stage. Don't ask me at the last moment. I am not a free bird who can accommodate any of your plans at any given time." Aamod told her in angry tone.

Mia was shocked to hear the tone of Aamod. He never talked to her in that tone. She thought he knew why she is so busy but today she realized that Aamod had never understood that. He was so engrossed in himself, that he never thought about why she couldn't give him time. If he would have understood then he would have helped her. Mia felt so helpless at that moment. She took all the responsibility and gave all freedom so that Aamod can focus on his career but he interpreted it differently and now he is blaming her. Mia was unable to hold her tears and she turned to other side and started sobbing into pillow. The pillow is the one who understood her sorrow and tried to comfort her.

The coldness between Mia and Aamod was increasing day by day. Earlier Aamod used to take weekends off but now he started working on all Saturdays, leaving no time for Mia. Sunday was the only holiday for him and that too he used to spend doing all his pending chores. Mia stopped asking him for anything and that created a communication gap between them. No one was sorry about their actions, both thought that they were right.

Relationships needs to be restored. If it get attacked by interloper it needs to be corrected and not to be left unnoticed. If it left unnoticed it gets more and more vulnerable and sometimes it's beyond healing. Someone needs to take a step back and wait for reaction of the partner. If a person wait for the other person to take a step back, sometimes no one withdraws and the relationship gets bitter and bitter.

The New Normal

As Aamod went to Hyderabad for his office tour, Mia felt so lonely on that day. But Jay called and invited himself for dinner that evening. Neil was cheerful in presence of Jay. He didn't stopped talking and jumping and just wanted to tell everything to Jay. That surprised Mia a lot as she never seen Neil so happy around Aamod.

Jay had cautioned Neil not to ask Mia question about anything. The reason he told him that she is still not well. Neil was very horrified after that accident to see his mom in hospital and he immediately agreed so as to make his mom well soon. But whenever he is with Jay he felt very secure and he forgot all his fears which made him a happy and cheery boy.

Next day Jay took Neil to mall and they spent the whole day there. Playing games and enjoying burger and ice cream, it was really a treat for Neil after such a long time. Anvi gave company to Mia at home as Jay didn't felt it right to left Mia alone at home.

"I heard you are going back to office from Monday?" Anvi inquired Mia

"Hmm. It's very boring to just sit at home. And then this memory loss thing bothers me a lot. So I thought it's better to keep myself occupied with some work." Mia replied.

"But are you feeling alright. It's just two weeks from the accident happened. Do you have that much energy?" Anvi showed her concern.

"I am going to give it a try. If I feel that I am not feeling right, I can come home. After all it's my office? Right." Mia said with a smile.

"Yeah. That's true. And Jay is there so nothing to worry." Anvi showed confidence.

"Hmm. I wonder. How Neil is so attached to Jay. I know Aamod never spent time with Neil, but still, I found Neil a lot comfortable around Jay. Neil is so much happy and chatty around Jay but the same Neil becomes quiet around Aamod. That bothers me. I remember I always used to say Aamod to be with Neil but he never listened to me and now see, his own son doesn't responds him well." Mia poured her heart out to Anvi. Anvi was confused what to say. She just sat quietly for few minutes.

"So have you decided what you will wear on first day of your office?' Anvi asked to change subject.

"Oh come on. This is not my first first day to office." Mia tried to ignore the question.

"It is for you. You are going to an environment which is new for you, so I say you must think it as your first day' Anvi tried to cheer up Mia

"It's not like people there don't know me. It's me who don't know anyone there." Mia was little tensed about joining the office.

"Still I feel you should be excited as if it's your first day of office. Let's decide your outfit for the Monday and Tuesday and all the week." Anvi grabbed her hand and pulled her towards bedroom.

They spend an hour or two selecting outfits for Mia. And Mia felt better and excited to join the office.

As Jay promised, he came to pick her up on Monday morning. Mia was wearing her favorite pestle pink color top with blue trousers. She accessorized it with stone earing and a bracelet. She looked as fresh as a dew drop on pink rose. As she never like to wore makeup she just highlighted her lips with light pink lipstick which made her smile brighter and kajal in eyes made her eyes look expressive.

"Good Morning, Looking pretty as always. All set?" Jay greeted her.

"Morning and thank you. This is all Anvi's choice. You know her. I am ready. Let's go." Mia grabbed her bag and gave instruction to Neelu about Neil and left for the office.

"Somehow this feels familiar to me." Mia spoke unknowingly.

"What feels familiar?" Jay cannot hide his pleasure in his tone.

"This, going to office with you. Umm. Do we always go together to office?" Mia said as if remembering something.

"Yes. You are right. We go together to office every day." Jay was very happy to hear it, as it is a good sign.

Mia took out the CDs from glove box, chose the Kishor Kumar Songs CD and played it on the Music system.

"Why there is no CD in system? You were not listening to music? This CD is always there in the system. This one is you favorite." Mia said again without any hesitation as if it's her usual habit.

"Now I will listen. Since you were in hospital, I forgot everything I used to do." Jay replied her. Jay was relieved to know that she remembers something. That's a good sign he thought and smiled

In the office Anirudha has made sure that Mia will receive a warm welcome from all staff. Everyone from staff was a bit nervous as they were aware of Mia's condition. But Jay have warned them to act normally with her as if nothing has happened.

Jay took Mia to their office which was on 10th floor. At the reception area there was big poster welcoming Mia. Receptionist Radha greeted Mia and handed her a pink rose's bouquet. Jay gave Mia a short tour of their office and introduced everyone to her and then they settled in their cabin. The cabin was big enough for two of them.

The combination of yellow, orange and white color of the cabin, giving the warm look. Back wall of the cabin holds a painting showing different shades of seasons. The wall in front of their chairs was made of half glass which gives enough light and clear view of the office. The glass was covered with blinds, to keep the privacy when required.

What Mia has in mind was her earlier agency. The big conference room, art department with lots of artists table. A different cabin for Client servicing personnel, her friends in account team and from art department. This office was totally different. Though she is working here for last couple of years, in this course of time the mode of operations has changed a lot. Everything looks so unfamiliar to her that she got confused and scared at the same time to handle all this. Jay looked at her and immediately understood what she is going though. He asked Madan to pour a strong coffee for Mia. Madan was aware exactly what kind of coffee Mia loves. He made one and knocked on the cabin door.

"Come in' Jay replied

"Coffee sir" Madan hesitated to offer it to Mia as she didn't asked for it.

"Thank you Mandan, keep the coffee on Mia's table. Don't forget the coaster." Jay said in playful tone

"Mia, just have some coffee, you will feel fresh. Madan knows the exact proportion for your coffee." Jay asked Mia cheering her up.

"Hmm" Mia took coffee mug in hand and glanced at Jay. After sipping one sip from that mug she felt so great, she smiled looking towards Jay.

"Mia, I know everything is unfamiliar to you now, but in no time you will get used to it. Don't keep yourself in confused state and just keep doing work. I am here to help you, to guide you. Anything that bothers you please feel free to talk to me, to ask me. I will try my level best to make sure you are comfortable. Please don't worry and be easy on yourself. Finish your coffee and will discuss how to take things forwards. OK" Jay again spoke to her so nicely that Mia felt that she can overcome all this.

"Mia, we are doing a new campaign for our client, you head that account, so I want you to be part of discussion. Just be there and if you want to give any inputs, don't hesitate. Actually I want you to lead the campaign as usual." Jay assured Mia and they both headed to conference room for discussion with other artists.

Conference room was big enough to sit six to eight people. It was bright and facing the front side of building. The fountain at the entrance of the building was visible from the conference room as it has full glass windows on that side. The road joining the main road and building was covered with trees giving a soothing look. The building was not very far from main road, but the trees were cutting all the noise and chaos of main road. The fountain, the greenery was giving the feeling of calmness to that building. Situated on the main road yet away from the chaos of the city.

Anirudha was assistant to Jay and Mia. He initiated the discussion by giving the introduction about the campaign. Jay took over after that and started explaining the team, what are the main requirement of the client. There were three other member in that team. The usual protocol was whoever idea is best will then lead the campaign. It was meant to give importance to everyone at once. The brighter one will get the credit. And everyone has a chance to prove themselves. The three were Ashutosh, Avani and Mukta. All were bright and young artists. Mia and Jay used to lead them as they were not much experienced. The discussion started and since the client was a jeweler, Avani and Mukta were more excited and have more ideas to present. Soon Mia took over the discussion and they finalize the concept. Mia corrected some points and asked Avani and Mukta to start the work. Mia seemed to be excited and in controlled with her work as if she hasn't been away.

After meeting she thanked Jay for having her in spite of her condition. Jay was more than happy to have her, but didn't mention that.

They finished their lunch and Mia started her computer and the operating came naturally to her. She was surprised by that, but some of our actions are so much tailored in subconscious mind that we are not aware of. The day went smoothly in office and Mia was happy that she still can work while Jay was happy that he got to spend so much time with Mia after such a long period. Jay Dropped Mia home and went to see Dr. Patel. He called him to report Mia's progress, and wanted to know what should be next course of action.

"Good evening Doctor" Jay greeted

"Good Evening" Doctor Patel replied with big comforting smile.

"Doctor, Mia joined office from today. At first she looked very scared and confused but as the day passed she seemed to be sorted and confident about her work."

"That's very good. See, that's the beauty of our brain. It may have blocked some of her years in conscious mind, but her sub conscious mind is all at work. She has full chances of getting her memory back."

"Doctor sometime I feel that she remembers some things about me, about our relationship from her face, I can make it, but in a flash she again gets blank. Why it is so?

"Hmm. You know she is in very difficult position. For her she is married to Aamod, and you are just her colleague. If at all she has some flashes of memory, she don't allow them to surface as you are not supposed to be anyone to her. Try to understand her point of way."

"But then if at all she get her partial or full memory back, will she accept it or she will not?" Jay was getting nervous as he know Aamod won't be able to continue with this arrangement for long.

"That will be depend on what part of memory she regains you know. If she regains only the part of your relationship she might not accept it, if she regains the memories about Aamod she might refuse to accept. It's really complicated. What I feel is that you start creating some situations which changed her life. Or which are very much important to her. Take her to the same places of her interest, or may create same situations happen before. That might help to trigger her memory." Doctor Patel was trying to help Jay to explain Mia's condition.

While driving back Jay was thinking what he should do, which will trigger her memory back to normal. He was thinking of number of options for it, but was not able to conclude on any one. He was so confused that he decided to call Anvi and take her help in this whole situation. Anvi stood thick with Mia in every single turn of her life. She was a strong woman and was very much involved in their life. It was Anvi who made them realize their feelings about each other.

Jay smiled after he remembered how she made him sit in front of her, and told him the truth about his own feelings. She was very much concerned about Mia now and always. She helped Mia through her time before and after divorce. Mia was totally broken down physically and mentally about that broken relationship. It was Jay and Anvi who helped her to face the truth and walk on her way. Jay had witnessed that condition of Mia and he didn't want her to go through that same pain again. He dialed Anvi's no and requested her to meet him next day.

Jay briefly told Anvi about his meeting with Doctor Patel and asked her to meet. That left Anvi confused as what must be the reason? Mia was her best friend since childhood. And Anvi had her back in her thick and thin time. Whether it may be her personal life or professional life. Anvi felt most happy when Mia got married to Aamod, and was devastated to hear about their decision to get separated. Anvi had witnessed each and every step of her life. Jay supported Mia and loved her very much. He bought back smile on Mia's face, he made her feel important again and both thanked Anvi for that because she is the one who made that happened. Anvi Still remember those days. After divorce Mia was sad for some days, but she joined her office and routine came back. She was all alone as she lost her parents in car accident. Then this divorce come up. But Mia stood strong in all these situations as she was aware that her kid Neil is totally dependent on her and she has to face the reality of life and marched forward for the betterment of her son. So she did. She confidently face the rest of the world and stood strong. And all the time Anvi was her strong pillar of support through losing her parents and losing her marriage. Anvi don't want to see Mia to face all those situations again which she has gone through post her divorce. She remembered the condition of Mia after the separation and divorce from Aamod.

Mia completely immersed herself in taking care of Neil and her job. She didn't have any kind of social life. Office home, home office that's it. In office Jay was her support. Jay never showed her sympathy for her divorce and Mia liked that. Jay always treated her as normal as any other collogue. She wanted to change her job, as to avoid sympathy from all her coworkers, but Jay assured her that he will take care of it and so did he. Working with Jay was a learning process. He was such good guide in all the aspects that the person who is seeking guidance always felt relaxed in his company.

A year passed by. Mia was not ready to get out of cocoon made by her. The organization asked them to visit their client in Silvasa. The client wants them to see his plant and office as he wants his office to have some designer's touch. Mia was not ready to go, she went to Jay and said

"Jay, I don't want to go there. Please take someone else."

"Mia you are lead artists for this client. You are the one who is aware of his choices. If you are not going then how will you execute the designs?" Jay was adamant on his decision.

"I know I lead this account, but I can't leave Neil and go out." Mia started giving excuses.

"Mia it's just question of one day. We are coming back on same day. It's not overnight excursion.

Neil always stays without you every day. You come to office and he stays there with babysitter. It's nothing different than that." Jay didn't understood what exactly going on Mia's mind.

"Actually I don't want to go anywhere." Mia finally said what she wanted to say.

"Mia, first thing, this is not picnic you are going to. So don't feel guilty about it. This is work and you are not going for some kind of enjoyment leaving Neil behind. And if at all you go for it, you have full right to enjoy your life. Isn't it? Why you are burying yourself in work and home. You are young, talented. Your marriage is over not your life. Live the life when it's time. Don't spend it inside four walls." Jay was trying to tell her the facts.

"Hmm. But give me some time. I will confirm it tomorrow." Mia said nervously.

"Mia I don't want you to live your life just because you are breathing. You must value every second of life. And if you don't enjoy life, what lesson you are giving to Neil. When he will grow up, he will also become a person who will bury himself in his work and will scare to enjoy. Because he will be looking up to you. Don't you want your son to live life fully and enjoy." Jay said in advisory tone.

Mia just nodded and keep doing her work. She thought how nicely this person says everything. Whatever he says, it felt correct. And he was right also. If I don't keep myself happy, how Neil will be happy person. After all, children always follow the path their parents walk. So what, I am divorced, that really doesn't mean my life is over. I should start over again. I must. For Neil's sake.

In the evening while going back home she called Anvi

"Hi"

"Hey, how are you? And where are you" Anvi greeted showing her pleasure.

"I am on my way back to home. How are you?"
"I am good. How are things at office? I am coming there this weekend. Let's meet and chat. I have lot to talk to you." Anvi was working in Pune for over a month on some project.

"Ok. Sure. Anvi, I want to talk to you regarding something." Mia hesitated a little as she was not sure how to start the topic.

"Oh come on, now now. Since when you have this hesitance while talking to me?" Anvi tried to made her comfortable

"My client wants me to visit his office in Silvasa. Jay is accompanying me. But I don't feel going. When I told him that I don't want to go, he was kind of upset"

"But why you don't want to go. It just Silvasa, and its work. And if at all you want to go for picnic, what's so wrong about it? Why you don't want to enjoy? Come on Mia." Anvi said in annoyed tone.

"You talk exactly like Jay. He was also lecturing me that my marriage is over and not life. I must enjoy and be happy otherwise what Neil will think and all. You both think same or what?" Mia was little surprised by what Anvi expressed

"What's wrong did he said then? He is right Mia. We all think that. You should not feel guilty about it. You are behaving as if you have lost your husband. It was divorce. The relationship didn't worked out. That's it. It happens. That doesn't mean you will not have good relationship in future. That does not mean you should stop living. How many times I told you this."

"Hmm. But divorce is divorce. I can't forget the good time we had. And I just keep thinking on where and what went wrong? That makes me sad."

"It's over now Mia. You tried, he tried but it didn't worked out. Now let it go. Don't think much about the past. Think about the present, the future. Try to be in present and be happy. Your relationship with Aamod was your past. Now you cannot reverse it. It's over. So just try to move on."

"I know you are right but it's very difficult for me."

"Well. Now listen to me. Just go for this office tour to Silvasa. When are you going and for how many days you are going? Do you want me to come and take care of Neil? I can come." Anvi pushed her to go.

"It's just a day. Will come back in the evening."

"OMG! Then what's bothering you. Go. Have your one day. My god this girl makes life so tough sometimes. Mia please go. And if you need any help from me, I am always there for you."

"Ok. I am going. Just relax. See you this weekend. Can't wait to meet you. Bye dear"

"Bye bye, and be yourself on this tour. Love you."

"Love you too." Mia disconnected and sigh in relief. After talking to Anvi she felt so much better. She decided to go to Silvasa

Next morning Mia confirmed with Jay about going to Silvasa. Jay asked the receptionist to make further arrangements. They were travelling two days after. Jay informed Mia to be ready at seven in the morning as he was going to pick her up from her home.

Jay came exactly at seven in the morning. Mia was getting ready by then, so she asked him to come upstairs and have some tea. Neil was up early that morning and was jumping around. Mia requested babysitter to come early, she was running behind Neil and pleading him to have his milk. Jay asked her to give the mug of milk and called Neil,

"Hey superman, come here"

Neil started looking at him with surprise in his big eyes and replied

"I am not superman, I am Batman"

"Oh, I am sorry batman. Please forgive me for calling you superman" Jay said dramatically with crying face. That made Neil laugh and he went near to Jay

"Why you are running away from your Bournvita? If Batman doesn't drink Bournvita how he will have energy to fight with joker?"

"Yes, Batman must drink milk to fight joker. Batman must have energy." Neil took the glass of milk and started drinking it. In between he was constantly talking about Batman. From where no one knows but Neil had become diehard fan of Batman. Always wanted Batman figurines, batman poster and every other thing with Batman picture on it. He kept asking questions about Batman to Mia and sometimes Mia get annoyed with his questions. But now she saw Jay and Neil talking about Batman and smile came on her face. At last someone is answering this little fellow with satisfying answer.

"Uncle, do you know where does Batman live?"

"Umm, I knew it, but I don't remember, can you help me to remember?" Jay asked him in such a tone that Neil got inspired about telling him.

"He lives in Gotham City and he helps people by fighting with Joker." Neil was too excited to talk about Batman.

"Oh yes, I knew that Gotham city and Joker always tries to destroy the city and Batman prevents him from it, right." Jay was talking to Neil not in baby tone, that gave Neil a confidence and he started talking to him as if they were friends and they are of same age. Mia was listening to their conversation and was surprised to see this side of Jay. The very formal and professional Jay was now talking to a kid in such a way that they were friends. Generally people talk with young kids in manner that they are talking to someone who is small and don't understand anything. But here Jay has giving Neil the feel that he is not kid but a person who has knowledge and is mature, that gave Neil a confidence and feel of older kid. That was little funny to watch, but that built the bond between them. Neil was more than happy to know a person who is interested in Batman. As of now the people he came in contact with, were either not interested in Batman or don't want to talk about it. But Jay didn't pushed him away by distracting from his Batman and gave him some more info. After a while Jay promised Neil that he will tell him more about his superhero when they meet next time and said bye. Mia placed a kiss on Neil's cheek while leaving for Silvasa. Neil happily waved them goodbye.

Jay and Mia started their journey for Silvasa. It was half an hour past seven.

"Sorry for late. I was planned everything for leaving at seven, but Neil didn't woke up and then everything ran out of scheduled time." Mia was little ashamed as they started late because of her.

"I can understand. He is just kid. Sometimes we need to adjust with them also. And we are not that late. We will reach there by eleven max. So don't worry. Our meeting is scheduled at 12. So we have enough time" Again this time Jay assured her and calmed down her anxiety.

"Thanks for understanding and not getting mad for late" Mia showed gratitude with smile.

"No need to say thanks. I know how tough is to handle young kids. And we are on time. So no worries." Jay smiled showing warmth.

"You get along with Neil very fast. I was not aware of that you are so good with kids."

"It's actually because I grew up with my nieces and nephews. And lot other children. I am the youngest in the family."

"Oh really. I can't believe that" Mia replied with surprise in her voice.

"What you can't believe, I am youngest or I grew up with children?" Jay's tone was little naughty.

"Yeah, actually both." Mia replied in a low voice.

"Why?"

"Hmm... You are very serious at work and that gave us feeling that you must be very strict and since you always have solutions for every problem, that gave impression that you must be the elder in your siblings. You know, the elder ones are always mature and knowledgeable. And the younger ones are naughty and childish as they were always been pampered."

"Oh.... You guess a lot. And what about you, were you the oldest or youngest?

"What do you think?" Mia replied with question.

"Oh, I can't guess. You only tell."

"I am the only child. No siblings."

"Oh… you don't look like." Jay said in surprise

"What is so different about single child?"

"Generally they are kind of self-centered as they are center of attraction in the family and always been paid attention to their needs. So the single child is always kind of attention seeker. Pampered and sometimes spoiled." Jay said in irritated tome.

"I took it as compliment then." Mia said in mischievous tone and they both laughed.

The journey took off on a lighter note and Mia felt relieved and stress free. The morning was pleasant and everything looking fresh. The darkness was over and the sunshine was giving hope of new beginnings to every part of nature which also comprise Mia. She was happy and feeling fresh after a long time. The black clouds of separation and divorce were moving away giving way to sunshine of hope and happiness.

After taking a short tea break they reached Silvasa on time.

#

Mr. Kulkarni, The client has took over the family business in recent times. The senior generation decided to hand over and give try to the younger generation. Mr. Kulkarni was in his late thirties, tall with fair skin and very enthusiastic with radiant green eyes that express intelligence. He wants to give a fresh look to his office and production unit to motivate his employees. The senior Kulkarni agreed to this idea and they asked him go ahead. Jay and Mia entered their premises. It was a bit old but the renovation work was in progress. The manager showed them way to Mr. Kulkarni's cabin.

"Good Day and welcome to Silvasa" Mr. Kulkarni greeted with broad smile.

"Good day sir. I hope we are on time" Jay politely replied to him

"Oh yes. You are perfectly on time. You must have started early."

"Yes, you can say that. But that was not a problem." Jay immediately responded.

Mr. Kulkarni offered snacks and tea. After refreshments he showed them all the facilities and explained his requirements. Mia noted down everything and her mind had already started working on the color, the graphics, and the messages. She was asking questions, giving suggestions. She was behaving like the earlier Mia, completely different. A confidence, that she can execute this job, was flowing through her veins reflected as glow on her face. Jay felt that and was very happy to see Mia back on track. Last year was very tough for her, she never let it reflect that in her work but the freshness had vanished from her face which was returning now. Change of place is what one needs to overcome the sorrows, Jay thought and smiled.

"So, I hope you have understood what I want?" Mr. Kulkarni asked both of them to see if they have any queries.

"Absolutely sir, we are clear on your approach. We will get back to you by the end of the next week with our suggestions and design ideas. I hope that is ok." Jay asked Mr. Kulkarni giving him a rough idea of deadline.

"Oh sure. That will be fine. We will be awaiting for the same." Mr. Kulkarni replied.

"On that note will take your leave sir." Jay shook hands with Mr. Kulkarni and asked for permission to leave.

"Yes. Of course but that will happen only after having lunch with us. I have specially reserve a space for all of us in one of the famous hotel of Silvasa. Try their food and I promise you will come to visit Silvasa only to relish on their food." Mr. Kulkarni laughed and insisted to have lunch.

The Hotel was not very classy type but was clean and airy. The smell of the food realized Mia and Jay that they were hungry. Mr. Kulkarni ordered typical kathiawadi food that was fantastic. The specialty was they were serving hot rotis dripping with pure ghee. The servers were serving hot and delicious food on plate. Loads of variety was served but Special dahikadhi and khichdi was the ultimate delight of the meal. After finishing their meal Jay said to Mr. Kulkarni that he will really visit Silvasa for this food. They all laughed and Mia and Jay started their journey back to Mumbai.

When they left the city behind and reached the highway, Jay turn on the music. The song first played was Zindagi ek Safar hai suhana by Kishore Kumar. While listening to that song, unknowingly Mia said

"How true this lyrics are. Seriously the life is really a journey and we really don't know what's going to happen next? Whether next day will bring happiness or not we don't know?"

"That is why we should live in the moment. Past we cannot change, future we don't know. What we have in our hand is present moment. So one should try to live and enjoy the moment. Which will make happy memories of past, which we can remember in future." Jay replied

"Thanks Jay for forcing me to come to this tour. Otherwise god knows when I would have tried to come out of the clouds of loneliness." Mia Sighed

"Whatever is happening was destined to happen Mia. We cannot change our destiny. Now today also you coming to Silvasa was destined, isn't it?" Jay asked

"True. But sometimes it is not easy to accept whatever happening with your life. I was never ever thought in my dreams that I will get separated from Aamod forget about divorce. We have beautiful relationship for more than ten years. I don't understand when and what went wrong which drifted us apart." First time after her divorce Mia was talking about Aamod with Jay.

"Hmm… Whatever happen was definitely very miserable, but why don't you think it otherwise. See, you only said you had beautiful relationship with Aamod for ten years, so admire those ten years. What I believe is, if you didn't get separated in that period you would have more bad memories than good ones. Which will have ruin everything. Now at least you can say that you have more good memories over that bad ones." Jay was trying to console Mia

"Hmm. Whatever. But I never wanted that to end. I believed in 'and they lived happily ever after" Mia was not convinced.

"Mia, I don't know what was the reason of your divorce, but I believe in the phrase whatever happens, happen for a reason. Just keep faith on something good is going to happen whatever difficulties one need to face. Whatever happen in our lives good or bad that's our perspective of looking towards the incidents. But all the incidents are happening, are to teach us, to make us better person, which results in the betterment of our future. That's what I completely agree on." Jay was very firm on his thinking

"I never disclose this to anyone. Aamod was seeing someone, and that's the reason of our divorce. I felt this very insulting as I was not able to give him that love which he needed. Or maybe, I was not a perfect match for him, or not a good person so he got attracted to someone else. This kills me. The rejection kills me. It hurts me that the person whom I loved so much, to whom I was the world, to whom I supported in every difficulties have distanced me. Left me for someone else. Why…. I want answer for this question. Where did I failed in that relationship? I cannot find the answer and it kills me from inside." Tears started rolling down Mia's cheeks. She was not able to control her emotions. After a very long time she was discussing her inability to maintain relationship. She was so stressed from inside, that the little topic vented everything out. Jay waited for some time and let her cry. He thought that would help to relieve some stress. After some time Mia calm down and apologized to Jay for her behavior.

"I am so sorry to break down in front of you like this. I am not like this."

"It's ok. No need to apologize. I can understand how stressed you are?" Jay said calmly.

"It's not me. I never cry in public, I never let me go over my emotions. I am in no need of sympathy. I don't know what happen."

"The song happen, I suppose." Jay said with little mischief in his voice. And that made Mia smile and thought, this person is really a gem. He understands me very well. For over a year he never asked me about my life and I am like a fool cried in front of him over my personal crisis. Mia was feeling ashamed of herself being so vulnerable.

"Don't need to be ashamed of yourself. I never discussed or asked you about your marriage or divorce as I didn't want to interfere in your personal space, and I thought you wouldn't like it. But that doesn't mean I was not concerned about it. I just thought that it was not my place to ask. But since you are sharing I have all my ears to listen to you." Jay showed his empathy.

Mia was surprised to hear him say that. How he knows what I was thinking? Is he a mind reader or psych or something? How one can be so perfect about what other person is thinking. She was stunned to hear.

"I understand what you must have gone through. The rejection must be the tough part for you because you don't like rejections. But what I will say to you is don't take it that way. Why you think that you are rejected, no one can reject anyone. It's his loss that you are not part of his life. He had lost you and not the other way. Sometimes we really need to think that whatever happened happen for something good. May be that was the life of that relationship. Remember the good times and try to forget bad ones. Try to move on with life remembering the happiness you gathered from that relationship. And see one has said happiness is inside you, nobody can give it to you and no one can take it from you."

"Jay, whatever you are saying is right. I get it. But still the question remains, what went wrong and why with me?" Mia was still not satisfied with the explanation

"You know one thing, God give difficulties to them who are strong enough to face them, to overcome them. You are strong, intelligent and confident. You can face this, so God chose you, so face the situation and as they say don't ask why me, instead ask 'Try Me'"

"Jay, this is easy to say "Try me" to console someone but it's not easy to face and say 'Try me.' I understand that you want to support me and give strength, but seriously I find it very difficult to forget, forgive and move on."

"Mia, who is asking you to forget, but yeah I will definitely ask you to forgive. Because unless and until you don't forgive, you cannot move on. And for Neil's sake you need to move on. I know how little one gets afraid if their parents are not happy, they think they are the reason for their parent's misery and they may lost their confidence. Neil is very sweet kid, don't do this to him. Already he must have lot of questions about his father, and he sees that you are also not happy, what must be going on in his mind. How much stress he must be carrying, have you thought about it?" Jay's tone was upset with concern of Neil.

"Hmm. My friend Anvi, she was also trying to say me same thing the other day. I agree with both of you. I have to think about Neil and his feelings. He is just a small kid who needs to be pampered and taken care of, and not to be worried about his parents. I will try my best to keep myself happy." Mia smiled forcibly.

"That's like a good girl. So keep smiling and the world will smile with you. And it's not just saying but the truth. Keep smiling and you feel the happiness and you spread the happiness. You know one thing, if you share a smile with a stranger, the person forgets his stress for that moment and tries to smile back. That's the power of a smile. So smile…." Jay stretch his thumb and first finger and put it on his mouth. He felt happy to hear that Mia is ready to try moving on and being happy.

Is this really happening in my life was Mia's first thought. Since separation, she buried herself so much in grief, that she somehow has forgotten how to smile, how to be happy. Divorce was very tough for her. The thought that Aamod will not be part of everyday life was killing her. The feeling, Aamod chose someone else to share his life over her was hurting her. She was not able to understand that where she was wrong, what wrong she has done, so Aamod stopped loving her, the thoughts were so intense at times that she forgot the timeline of day. She was standing tight on the ground because of Neil, he was the only ray of light in her dark days. Now she have to think about the psychology of that little one and need to come out of her cocoon which she weaved with her sorrow and spread her wings towards the hope of life.

The journey back to home felt very pleasant to Mia as Jay has given her a new thought, a new way to look to her life, a new hope with face of Neil. She was feeling relaxed. The stress, the burden has been lifted from her shoulder. She didn't realize it that time, the magician was Jay, his little talks and his company. But that journey tied them in some kind of sweet, nurturing bond.

#

Jay came out of his thoughts as Anvi waved on his face

"Where were you?" Anvi said in curious tone.

"Oh, nothing just lost in thoughts." Jay shook his head while replying to Anvi.

"I can see that, but you were so lost that you didn't notice my presence. I was waving you from across the road like a fool." Anvi sarcastically commented.

"Oh, sorry I didn't saw you coming."

"That's what I am asking where were you in your thoughts?" Anvi repeated the question.

"And by the way, yesterday what did Dr. Patel suggested about next step?" there was concern in Anvi's voice.

"For that only I asked you to meet me today. First let's order something, what will you have" Jay asked.

"I will have coffee."

"What did doctor said?" Anvi was curious to know.

"Dr. Patel suggested that we should recreate some situations which happen to be the life changing for

Mia. I need your help for that matter. It will not possible for me to do that on my own, I need your help to sort out such situations." Jay said in confused tone.

"Of course. I am always there. We will discuss about it. I know that the divorce thing is very much life changing situation for Mia, but that didn't happen in a one shot, it was like they started drifting away pass before the actual divorce so that will not help us solve this. Umm, I think you and Mia went on client visit to Silvasa, after that her approach towards life changed a lot. She started to smile again." Anvi was thinking about those days.

"That thought just bounced back to me. I was lost in those thoughts when you came." Jay replied with smile.

"Let's arrange some office visit to outstation and try to recreate that situation. May be that will help her to remember some things." Anvi said hopefully.

"Yeah, that came to my mind, but I am not sure how she will react to it. I remember last time also she did not show much interest to go on that site visit." Jay was not sure how to convince her.

"Leave that to me. I will take care of it, if she gives any excuses. I will talk to her. If she refuses to come, she will definitely going to discuss that with me." Anvi said in assurance.

"Ok then let's start mission office tour." Jay said in happy tone as he really wanted to go out with her and spend time.

"Not mission office tour, its mission get our Mia back." They both high fived and laughed.

"I will start working on it tomorrow." Jay was very happy with thought of going somewhere out with Mia.

"Keep me posted" Anvi reminded Jay and took off.

Reminisce

"It's been three weeks Aamod. Is there any difference in Mia's health? Has she remembered anything at all?"

Putting the coffee mug down forcefully, Aarohi expressed her irritation about the situation. Every time when Aamod leaving to stay with Mia, Aarohi was disturbed and felt insecure. She never wanted Mia to be a part of her life with Aamod and for that matter she always avoid to meet Neil and doesn't allow Aamod to meet him either.

She was not at all comfortable with the idea of Aamod been staying with Mia. She was insecure about the thought that what if Aamod develops soft corner for Mia, and what if she never get back her memory. This horrifying thought and uncertain future was making her nervous to the core.

"It's not in our hand Aarohi. The thing is Dr has insisted not to tell her anything or otherwise it will get overwritten on her memory and there are chance that she will never remember anything. So it's like wait and watch situation. I know, I am not able to spend time with you, but its matter of just few more days. Please understand." Aamod felt hopeless to explain.

"Aamod, if I had some sort of certainty about the situation then I wouldn't have minded. But as far as I understand, there is no fixed period for this. It may take weeks, or months. What am I supposed to do? Do you want to keep me waiting for infinite period of time? That's not possible. I want to know, when you are going to solve this, which has no importance in my life. Why should I compromise on my peace of mind for somebody's concern?"

"Why are you losing it? I don't understand. It's not like I am going to stay there forever. And before taking this decision I did took concern from you. Since you agree to this, I went ahead for staying there."

"As if you gave me any choice. The way you asked me, I didn't have any choice but to say yes. And at that time I was not prepared and thought about this. I am realizing it now. You shouldn't have agreed to this. Why did you asked me, you could have denied it in the first place? You wanted to do this, but you need someone else's confirmation so that you will not be blamed. If you wouldn't have agreed then, my concern wouldn't have required" Aarohi was very angry with the situation. She was feeling hopeless and frustrated.

"You have to give me some confirm time, till when you are staying there and when I can expect you back home. I cannot be in this hanging position forever. Just tell me and this discussion is over." Aarohi gave the ultimatum to Aamod.

"I really don't know Aarohi. But today I will speak with Jay and let you know."

"See again you are going to ask Jay. No. I want you to give him certain date and that's it. You are not bound to do this, don't forget you are doing favor and not like this is kind of your duty or something. Or did you don't want to come back to me, you want to stay there permanently?" Aarohi's frustration was not turned into her anger.

"Ok. I will tell Jay, that this is the last week I am spending there, then he is on his own. Whether or not Mia get her memory back. Happy now? I will back home next week for sure. Is that ok?' Aamod put his both hands on Aarohi's shoulder to give confirmation that he is finally agreed to what Aarohi was suggesting.

"You are doing this with your own will, not because I force you to do, right?" Aarohi was still not sure about what Aamod conveyed to her.

Aamod was confused as how to talk to Jay about this. But he has to, because now it was getting difficult to handle Aarohi and he don't want his relationship to suffer. At the end, Mia and Jay belonged together and Aarohi deserves to be with him. But the toughest part of talking this out has to be executed by him. Which he was finding difficult. Finally he dialed Jay's number and asked him to meet him before reaching to Mia's house.

When Aamod's number displayed on the screen Jay lost a beat on thought that Aamod is calling that he will not be able to continue with the current set-up. The thought of Jay was not far from the reality. Aamod gave the ultimatum. Since Aarohi was not that comfortable with Aamod staying at Mia's house, Aamod confronted that he cannot continue to stay there more than a week. In that time Jay needs to do something for Mia's memory to get back to normal or he need to tell her the reality. Aamod offered his help to talk to Mia about the current scenario and telling her about their divorce. But that has to be happened in this week only.

Jay was not sure about telling Mia the truth before he is sure about her remembering something about their relationship. What if she didn't admit that it was the truth, and what if she never feels the same for him. The main fear for Jay was that Mia doesn't remember the fact about their relationship, how much he loves her and how much she loves him back. It all about the feelings, the emotions the bodings they have together that mattered. It's not about Mia accepting the fact that she has been divorced and now in relationship with Jay, it's about the warmth, the passion she must feel, that is more important that just accepting the fact about the reality. But now Jay had no time for that. He needs to act in such a way, so that the shock will be less effective for her.

Aamod spent the weekend with Aarohi and came back. Mia was now little disturbed with Aamod's behavior and his weekend schedule. From the day she was back from hospital, Aamod was avoiding her as much as he can. He was coming late from office, then giving excuse of some client's urgency kept working till late and the slept on couch. Every weekend he has some meetings or some work to be finished or some tours arranged in such a way that he will be back either on Sunday or Monday morning from where he directly went to office. It was not acceptable for anyone. She decided to talk through about this with him. After dinner when Aamod was about to open his laptop, Mia entered living room after putting Neil to bed and said, "We need to talk Aamod"

"Um, about what?" Aamod was surprised with the tone of Mia.

"About you avoiding me and Neil"

"Well, why do you think that I am avoiding you?" Aamod was nervous as he was not sure what is there on the plate.

"Oh, this is not avoiding then what exactly is. Since I am back from hospital, I am seeing this weird behavior or schedule of yours. On every weekend you are busy, every day you try to come late and then post dinner just start working and the spend rest of the night here on couch. Not a single time, since I have lost my memory you have taken effort to help me to remember things or you have visited the hospital with me. Every time Jay is there for me and not you. You are my husband and you are supposed to take care of me and Neil and not Jay.

He is nice fellow and helping me out, but I cannot keep asking him favors every now and then. Why you are not trying to understand?" Mia spoke in one breadth and looked at Aamod suspiciously.

"Now if he is offering helping hand how am I supposed to stop him? And I am busy as my project is going on floor within a week, so there are lot of last minutes details that needs my attention. What should I do, should I leave my job, career and start following you? Is that what you want? This job is very important for me. You please try to understand." Aamod replied which was half-truth. How he was supposed to explain to her why he was spending nights on couch.

"Oh, really. Now your job is more important than you wife, your family? What if I never get my memory back? I have lost eight years of my life, don't you understand gravity of this situation? What I am going though? How am I coping with this? Do you ever bother to know about that? You don't have time to talk about it, to discuss about it. I am just fed-up about this behavior of your's. I cannot take this kind of negligence you are displaying. I don't deserve this. I want someone to take care of me, to talk to me through this path on my problem, to hold my hand and assure me about being there for me in every situation. Unfortunately or fortunately, I have one good friend with me all this time, but I wanted you to be part of it. This cannot be done Aamod. I am not buying this at all. You have to sort out your priorities. What you want more?" Mia was furious to hear the explanation from Aamod.

"I have to work on this project as I am working on this for a very long time. I am sorry that this happen with you but I cannot leave the project in between and be there with you. So you just chill and wait.' Aamod didn't know what to answer to he just blurred something out.

"Fine. I understood. Good night. Now I need to think about this" Mia said furiously and left the room.

While lying down on bed Mia had a déjà vu feeling, that she had same kind of fight with Aamod a sometime before and then she left the home next day with Neil. But what happened after that, she could not remember that. She tried to, but then a shot of pain came through her head and she cried in pain. As doctor has advised her to take a pill in case of such pain she opened the bottle and swallow the pill with water. Within minutes she felt dizzy and fall asleep.

Next morning as usual Aamod left for the day early without any hesitation about last night. Mia got more furious seeing this behavior and she called Anvi.

"Hi, good morning. How come you remembered me so early in the morning?" Anvi replied in playful voice.

"Hi, good morning. And hey I don't forget you, so there is no question about remembering you?" Mia replied in low voice.

"Hmm, what happened? Is everything ok? You don't sound ok." Anvi asked with concern.

"I don't know what to say? Aamod is behaving so weird day by day. It is very frustrating and he does not talk to me properly, don't answer my questions, even he is not taking any efforts to show at doctor's appointment. Just avoiding me as usual." Mia spitted out everything that was dancing on her mind.

"Hmm. Did you talked to him about this?" Anvi took a pause before replying as she was unsure how to respond.

"Yep. Yesterday I asked him. He replied that he is busy on some project and cannot leave that project in between. But that's not the point I called you. After that arguments with Aamod, I had a déjà vu like feeling. Same this situation has happened earlier also and then I took off from his house with Neil. But I don't remember what happened afterwards. When I tried to remember that, there was a sharp pain shot in my head and I went blank. So I just swallowed the medicine doctor prescribed and went to bed. I wanted to ask you, did I really left Aamod and went somewhere else. You must be aware of it, I am sure. So I need you to help me on this."

"Mia do you remember anything other than this? This is some news. Don't you think?" Anvi tried to avoid the question.

"Hmm. But that is not answer to my question Anvi. Did this ever happen?"

"Yeah, you came to me with Neil one night after fight with Aamod and stayed with me for a while. But this you don't remember, right?" Anvi asked her impatiently.

"I remember the fight and leaving home, nothing else yet. Don't share this with anyone now. Let's wait and see what else I can remember and then will disclose, I don't want to up the hopes on anyone regarding this." Mia cautioned Anvi.

"OK. How are you feeling now? Is your headache still there, should we need to visit doctor?"

"No, I am fine now. Still angry about Aamod's behavior but health wise I am fine. No need to go to doctor. So when can you meet me? Let's go for dinner as earlier we used to go. Let's have some fun." Mia changed the topic instantly.

"Sure, will go this week end to our favorite place"

"At Socials" Mia said in joyful tone.

"Yeah, we are going to have so much fun. See you on Saturday then."

"See you on Saturday. Bye." Mia disconnected the call.

The whole day Mia was upset and was in hope that Aamod may call her to apologize or at least to ask her about her mood. But he didn't call and now Mia was getting more and more angry. There Jay was noticing the difference in the Mia's behavior but he did not asked her as he was in different zone of thinking about his next move to accelerate the things which will help Mia with her memory. He was thinking about a trip to client's warehouse which was at Daman. The Silvasa visit was the first step when Mia shared her personal story with him. And that might triggered her memory.

Around afternoon coffee break Jay started the topic about visiting the client at Daman

"Mia, that Kaizen people want us to visit there warehouse. I was thinking may be in couple of days we both visit them."

"Hmm. Can you put a light on this as I don't know why we are visiting them?"

"Right. Actually they want to remodel their office and just want some inputs from us. Their interior designer has asked us to join the meeting. It's like joint venture with the interior designer. We will be co-working with them."

"Hmm. But do we also execute such type of jobs? I mean, it's not related to advertising I suppose?" Mia was really in bad mood and that was showing in her tone.

"Hmm. True but sometimes if client want our inputs other than advertising then I think we should do it, for the sake of the relation with client. And this is not first time we are doing, we have done this earlier too." Jay said in convincing voice.

"Which obviously I don't remember. I just don't know what things I am missing in my life. I am so tired about this situation and sometime feel that this is never going to get any better." Mia breathed out rubbing her forehead with both of hands.

Jay felt so helpless, he just couldn't watch her like this. But to fix this all, he has to decide about that trip now, and he cannot waste more days, so he continued with the conversation.

"I understand your position. Let's go to Daman and visit this client. You can use this for change of atmosphere from your routine and may be that will you help you be feel refreshed."

"I don't know about that Jay. But if it's important for our company then we should go. When are you planning to go?" Mia tone was gloomy.

"I was thinking of visiting there on this Wednesday. Will start early morning, reach there by 11, finish the meeting and reach back by 7 or 8. It's hardly 3-4 hours journey. So if you are Ok with this schedule then I will inform them today and fix up the meeting." Jay was more than happy after Mia's approval.

"Anything which you find appropriate Jay. I don't have any problem any day this week."

"Ok then. This Wednesday we are going to Daman."

Mia was lost in her thoughts so much that, she did not noticed the change in behavior and tone of Jay. She finished her coffee and turned towards her monitor.

It was like déjà vu feeling for Jay, when he reached to pick up Mia around 7 am in the morning. But the scene was not the same. Mia was ready and Neil was still in his bed sleeping. Mia was wearing a sky blue kurta which has small white flowers print. She paired that with while pant and white dupatta. She wore small white stone earring and a watch to accessories her look. In that simple attire she was looking gorgeous like a jasmine flower, fresh and pleasant. But her face was telling some other story. Her face was not showing any signs of freshness or happiness, yet she was calm and in control.

"Hey, you ready?" Jay greeted her with smile

"Hmm. Ready. Let's go and reach there on time. I just say bye to Neil and then we are ready to go." Mia went inside came back in a minute.

"Who is there with Neil?" Jay didn't saw Neelu around so he was little concerned.

"Oh, Neelu is there. She is downstairs to get some veggies. She will back soon. No worries. We can start." Mia took her bag and nodded to Jay.

Jay started the car and the CD started playing song Pyaar diwana hota hai, he paused the song and looked towards Mia to see any changes in here mood but no, she wasn't paying attention to the song, she was lost in her thoughts.

"If you want to listen to some other music, just select the CD and put it on. I was listening to these songs yesterday, that's why this started playing."

"Oh that's fine. Even I like Kishor Da's songs. So let's listen to this one only." Mia was definitely not in choosing her songs or listening to them. She was still thinking about her relationship status with Aamod. They were still not talking and Aamod didn't even tried to console her or pacify her or apologized to her for his behavior.

"We have to drive for around two and half hours. Aren't you interested in some road trip music which will make the journey more enjoyable?"

"Umm, not really. I am ok with any music or no music." Mia said very irksomely.

"Hmm, fine" Jay didn't find any words about what to say, he wanted this trip to be like the one they had years before. But he didn't want to stress anything on Mia, so he just started the car.

It was November morning, very pleasant and soothing. The sun has risen and it was breezy morning. Not the chill breeze but the pleasant one. Once they touched the highway the city traffic was gone and car took good speed. There was complete silence in the car. Only the noise of cars passing by was coming through closed windows. That silence was killing Jay. He wanted to talk to Mia so much. Wanted to know how she is feeling, he wanted her to ask him how he is and how he is doing. If this was normal Mia then they would have been listening to some music and the discussing about songs, music and what not. Mia was a person who loves to talk, she has lot of subjects and interest to talk about. Well-read and interests in almost everything from movies to travel to books to music. She has N number of topics to chit chat and Jay pretty much enjoyed that. This silence of Mia made him little sad and thoughtful about what exactly is going in her mind. Jay is also in tension what if Mia doesn't remember, Aamod was not ready co-operate any more as Aarohi has given him ultimatum. If Aamod moves out of the picture then he has to tell Mia about their relationship and that's where he was scared, what if she didn't accept and just walked away from him. So this is his chance to give Mia some clues about it. Jay and Mia both were thinking about relationship status but one is trying to revive the relationship while other one was thinking about the reviving the relation which was over few years back.

They reached Daman around eleven am. As Jay had already informed Mr. Waghela about Mia and requested him and his team to co-operate him to plan it accordingly, Mr. Waghela and his team were ready. They greeted them and walked though their office to show where they need some improvements. Mia was taking notes in her mind as well as on her notepad while taking the tour. She also suggested some changes and asked them if they can carry a theme. For which Mr. Waghela showed interest.

Jay thought, when any job comes across this girl just tosses her personal tragedies aside and gets passionate with work and the results come out pretty good. Mia, never ever you show any indication of your health or mental condition or your family problems when it comes to your work. A perfect example how to part professional and personal life. Even Mr. Waghela must be thinking whether I was wrong about what I told them. Jay smiled thinking about that, and Mia caught that and raise her eyebrows and smiled back. Looking her smiling Jay shook his head and he smiled little more.

The office tour and meeting was over by lunch time. Post lunch they said goodbye to Mr. Waghela and headed back.

Again when Jay started the car, same song started playing and both smiled looking at each other. After the meeting Mia was feeling good may be because of the discussion or because of the outing but for some time she forgot about Aamod and his behavior. She was in light mood and when Jay pause the song she said she wants to listen to the songs.

"Let's listen to some music. While coming we came totally in silence." Mia said in playful tone

"Hmm. You only didn't wanted to listened to it"

"When did I said I don't want to listen?" Mia questioned and Jay looked at her doubtfully

"You said music or no music"

"That doesn't mean no music. I wasn't in mood to select the music, I was ok with whatever was playing but you paused it and then never played it back" Mia said in convincing tone

"Oh My God. You are unbelievable. Because of you I drove two hours in complete silence. Now you have to pay for it. Now you will sing for two hours as punishment." Jay tone was mischievous

"Ha ha ha, I not going to sing just because you misunderstood. Did I say no music, what I said was music or no music. So if you wanted to listen you should have listen" Mia replied mischievously.

They drove back chatting and talking but the reason of this road trip was not achieved as Mia neither said anything about the last trip nor any memories bounced back

Jay is now more and more tensed about the condition of Mia. He is trying is level best to do so, but nothing was fruitful. He arranged dinners to their favorite places, he took her to places where they have beautiful memories, but nothing was hitting off to her. And this was turning into some kind of nervousness to Mia. Aamod was not spending time with her, and Jay was taking her for dinners and outings which made her think that Jay is showing pity on her and trying to fill the emptiness caused by Aamod's absence. And that's irritating for her. Things are going south, and it wasn't really working out the way Jay thought.

A week after their Daman trip, Aamod called Jay.

"Hi, Jay."

"Hi Aamod, how are you doing?" Jay's nervousness was showing in his voice.

"Not good Jay. You see, I am just tired of sailing in these two boats. Mia's condition is not improving and Aarohi has asked me to come back home this Saturday. I want to help Mia as much as possible but now I cannot ask Aarohi for any more favors. She is too much insecure about this from the beginning and now she has lost her patience. I can't blame her also. She has shown a lot of courage till now, but now she is becoming aggressive as there is not guarantee about when the things will get normal for Mia. So please forgive me. I am going back home this weekend."

"Hmm. I totally understand your situation Aamod. And I am very much thankful to you and Aarohi as both of you supported me so much in this. You could have stepped out if you wanted to, you don't need to do all this. But for me, for Mia you tried to help so much. I don't know what to do next but can you do a little favor for me?"

Another favor, Aamod felt so much burden about what he is going to ask.

As there was no response from other side, Jay continued

"Nothing much I am asking. Just when you are packing things up, pack when Mia is not at home. And just move them out. And on Friday tell her that you are going on office tour for some days and that time just carry one bag, so she will not suspect about anything."

"But what when I will not return after days? What will you do then?" Aamod was surprised to hear what Jay suggested.

"Will see, what to do at that time. I am just thinking about one step at a time. I don't want her to get disturbed thinking about you are moving out"

"Hmm. Ok. You are right in a way." Aamod agreed.

"Let me know if you need any help to move your things and I am seriously very much thankful to you and Aarohi for the support you offered" Jay assured Aamod, that things are ok with him.

"Just take care of Mia. She deserves to be loveed and I hope she will get her memory back soon." Aamod got emotional while saying this.

On Thursday while having dinner, Aamod spoke to Mia

"Mia, don't get upset. I am going to Hyderabad again for about two weeks. The project is about to start and I need to be there for last minute details"

"Hmm. What can I say? You and your work. And I even can't say that I will accompany you. My work needs me here. If you need to go then how am I supposed to stop you?" Mia replied in cold tone which made Aamod a bit nervous.

"I am going tomorrow directly from office." Aamod declared.

"Fine." Mia replied and Aamod understood that she is upset a lot. But now he didn't have any choice. He is acting as per Jay's direction. He thought, whatever happens now Jay will take of that.

Next day morning Aamod was is double mood. One way he was going back home to Aarohi and now he don't have to answer her as well as Mia, so that made his mood a bit lighter. But on the other hand, he was leaving Mia and was not sure how she will cope with it and what is going to happen next about her condition was making him a bit nervous. While having breakfast, he was in lighter mood. Looking at his behavior Mia thought that going away from house is making him feel lighter, is he happy to be away from me, from Neil? And that thought made her angry but she didn't showed it. Looking at Mia, Aamod got awkward as he understood that Mia is angry and he was not sure what he should do about it. Then he thought, I am not going to see her again soon, so by the time I see her, she might have cooled down.

Aamod left for office and Mia broke down. The tears started falling down her cheeks. She was not able to control herself. The thought of Aamod going away for so many days and that too without concerning her, was killing her. She just could not accept this. How a person can leave his wife and son, for so many days and that too when his wife was not well. Mia was crying and was not able to control her emotions. After a while she settled and washed her face with cold water and started getting ready for office. She was not in shape to go to office but she was aware that if she sits home, then she wouldn't be able to control her emotions and that Aamod's memory, the anger about his behavior will made her more and more vulnerable. The best way is going to office, the work, the people will keep her busy and she can bury her emotions and that will help her to get to normal at once.

When Mia reached office, Jay immediately noticed that she must have cried a lot as her eyes were swollen. But as usual he didn't poke her with any questions. He just smiled and pointed at his own eyes and her eyes with raising his eyebrows. Mia got the message. She smiled back and shook her head in reply, and got back to work. She was right, she forgot about Aamod in no time and was normal by the lunch time.

The week passed, Aamod hardly called her in that week and they spoke very little when he called. Mia was not sure about Aamod's behavior, and she did not want to discuss this with anyone. She was restless all the time from inside but didn't allow her emotions to surface. Mia was the women who never in need for sympathy. Jay was aware of her situation but he never mentioned it to her as he knew that Mia will not like it and if she wants to share she will, but otherwise asking her will be poking in her private space for her. For him, it was very difficult to keep himself away from her problems, from her sorrows but it was the time that was not allowing him to do so. For Mia, Jay was just a friend, a good one, but as far as Jay knew Mia, she would definitely not like anybody entering in her private space. Jay was also restless, but alike Mia he also did not allowed his restless to surface. Both of them were acting normally and that is hurting both of them from inside. The week passed and it felt like a long time has passed for both of them.

Friday Jay received call from his sister Sheena

"Hi Jay, how are you doing?"

"Good I suppose. How are you?" Jay answered in low tone

"No improvement in Mia's condition?" Sheena showed concern

"Not yet, but I am hoping for the best. If she didn't recover then only thing we can do is to tell her, and to see whether she accepts the fact or..." Jay was skeptical about the fact that how Mia will react when they broke the reality to her.

"Hmm. I know it is very sad and difficult time of your life. But anyways life goes on. We have to face the things that life throws at us, isn't it?" Sheena was trying to pacify Jay

"Hmm, But for how long. I don't know? Sometimes I fear this story of mine will not come to a happy ending."

"If the story doesn't end happily then the story is not finished my brother? You have to keep the story running until it reached the happy ending." Sheena told him definitively.

"Hope so. So why you called?"

"We are going on camping tomorrow. Kids wants you to join us. We are going with nice group of people for camping, will be living in tents by lakeside, will do star gazing and camp fire and barbeque etc. I want you to come with us. You have been much tensed lately. You will have some different group of people to spend time with" Sheena forced him to come.

"No Sheena, I can't leave Mia alone on weekend. Aamod is not coming back now, and I think she is aware of this situation somehow. She is a lot disturbed the whole week though she didn't showed it, I know. Now I cannot left her alone for the weekend, thinking about Aamod and getting more depressed."

"Dear, she has to face the reality sooner or later. And I think let her be alone for some time. Give her some space to think about it. Who knows that might help her to remember the past. And I think let her miss you, let her understand that what is life when you are not around. That might trigger the recovery. And besides if you also spend some time with other people, you might get fresh start on how to help her to recover, or find a solution on this problem. A fresh air and different people than usual helps sometime to think out of the box. So what do you think?" Sheena was not wrong.

"Hmm. What you suggest is also correct. Let me think about it." Jay was convinced by Sheena's words.

"Oh come on. Don't think now, pack your bags and just come." Sheena was now impatient about this trip

"Hmm, Ok, fine I will come. Let me inform Mia about this, and I will join you. Just text me the details and share the location, I will directly come there." Jay couldn't reject Sheena proposal.

"No, I am coming to pick you up tomorrow morning at 8. Be ready." Sheena doesn't want Jay to give any excuses at last moment.

"Oh, you don't trust that I will come?" Jay's mood has been lighter by now

"Yes, you are absolutely right. So see you tomorrow morning at 8. Be ready. You are going to have a beautiful weekend. See you, bye" Sheena disconnected the phone.

Jay dialed Mia's number to inform her about his camping tour but it didn't get connected. He left her message informing about the camping and that he will be back by Sunday lunch.

Next morning again Jay tried to call Mia but this time she didn't pick up the phone. Again he left her message. Going out for two days without speaking with Mia, made him restless for some time. But when Sheena arrived with her kids, in their company he just got caught up with them and then the thought of not talking to Mia got aside. The idea about living in tent under the sky made kids overjoyed which made them keep asking questions about the whole camping trip.

Mia was awake till late earlier night. Around four - four thirty she fall asleep. And then that resulted in the late morning start. Since it was holiday for Neil also, they started their day late with brunch. Neelu has made tasty parathas. Neil was cheerful as always. While having breakfast he asked Mia about Jay

"Mama, is Jay uncle visiting us today?" Spending time with Jay was most enjoyable for Neil. And since Mia has lost part of her memory, spending time with her was more stressful for Neil

"Umm, I don't know. He didn't talk about it yesterday." While talking to Neil, Mia checked her phone. And she saw his missed call and voice mails.

"Oh, Neil, Jay uncle went for camping today morning. He called me but I overslept so didn't got chance to talk to him."

"I also want to go camping, why didn't he took us with him?" Neil was upset as Jay didn't took him

"He is going with his family. And why would he took us everywhere he go?" Mia tried to convince Neil. Neil didn't said anything, but he wanted to say, ma we are his family.

"Ma if we can't go camping can we go somewhere out today? Please, please ma let's go someplace where I can play lots of games and we will also eat there." Neil dramatically begged. Mia laughed on his drama and said

"You are such a drama king, who will say no to this face? Let's go. But do you know any such place, as you know for me I haven't been anywhere in nearly eight years, my memory" She pointed at her head and raised her eyebrows while asking.

"Don't worry mama. We used to go this mall almost every moth. I will take you there. We can also visit the snow world there. They provide us snow suits and we can spend an hour at that place. It is so chilled in there, like we are sitting in fridge. And I can also play at play zone over there. You can also play with me, there are lot of games which we can play together. Let's go, let's go." Neil was overjoyed with the thought of going out.

"Ok, and where is this place? I need to book cab to go there. Finish your breakfast and get ready fast, so that we can spend more time there." Mia said to Neil while picking up her plate and glass.

"Neelu, don't make anything for lunch or dinner. I and Neil are spending the whole day out so will have something there. You take leave today. Just finish the dishes and help Neil to get Ready and then you can leave." Mia asked Neelu while keeping the plate in the sink.

Mia and Neil reached the mall by noon. It was on hours distance from home. Very first thing they did was they book the tickets to the snow park as Neil was very excited about it. Luckily they got tickets of immediate slot. The snow park management explain them the rules about what to avoid inside. Inside temperature was set to -2 to -3 degrees, for that the park provided visitors the fur coats, gloves and boots according to the size and visitors have to wear them before entering the park.

The Snow Park was actually a big hall with the minus temperature setting. When the doors opened, a chilly breeze hit them. Inside the park there was a skating rink. Neil wanted to try that so Mia took him there and helped him wearing skates. It was not easy to stand on the skating rink with those skates. At the very first attempt they both fell down badly and both burst into laughter. Then helping each other they stood up and with the help of the rod which was on the sides of the rink and they started walking holding that rod. It was fun and it was difficult. After some time some more people join and the same thing was happening with all of them. It was really a funny to watch.

After a while they felt very cold, to keep visitors warm, the park has arranged one room which has at 18-20 degrees temp. They both went to that room for some time and again come back to park.

There was a place where they manage to keep the snow where people can actually play in that snow. Mia and Neil started making snowman in the snow and suddenly Mia made a ball of snow, Neil asked her why she is doing a ball, it is not needed, and she threw the ball on Neil and laughed mischievously.

"This is the reason I was making ball mister." And she ran away from him.

"You have done very big mistake madam. Now it's my turn" Neil said while making snow ball and ran behind Mia. And at the same time it was time for snowfall. A real kind of snow started falling from the ceiling and it was a moment to cherish. Experiencing snowfall naturally was different story but this artificial snowfall was also very thrilling.

At one corner there was also a slide, of which the end was in snow. Neil saw that and ran towards the slide. Some adults were also enjoying that slide. Neil forced Mia to take the slide and Mia did take it. She felt little embarrassed first time but while sliding down in the snow, she felt the happiness. She felt like the child inside her is waking up and is smiling. She did tried the slide for some time.

The hour flew by so fast and it was time to exit the snow park. The bell rang to announce that time of visiting was over and everyone started walking towards the exit. Some people do want to spend till the last minutes, so the bell rang again as final warning and the management people started requesting visitors to exit the park. Neil and Mia both were cheerful and chatty. They changed their clothes and return them back. The noses and cheeks of both them turned red and both pointed each other. They had a loads of fun and also were very hungry after this hour long fun in Snow Park.

Mia took Neil to food court. Both of them collected their food and found a table near window. Neil was very excited about this whole mall trip. He was talking continuously about his school, about his friends, about his teachers. And Mia was listening very carefully as she wanted to know everything about him. They both were enjoying their food. Neil declare that from there he wants to visit the game zone. Mia nodded and asked him to finish his food first. Mia was desperately in need of coffee, she asked Neil to wait at the table while she will bring the coffee.

Mia ordered her coffee and waiting at the counter for the coffee to be served. She was just looking around as everything was new for her. Suddenly she spotted a person who was looking similar to Aamod from behind. She just shook her head and thought she is thinking a lot about Aamod and that is the reason she think that person is Aamod, because Aamod was in Hyderabad. But... She looked again carefully and noticed that he was not alone, he has a company of a girl and definitely they were couple as Aamod has put his hand on her shoulder and she was very comfortable. The body language clearly suggesting that they are more than friends. Mia was shocked and confused. What the hell is going on here? Who is that girl with Aamod? Who is that girl? To get those Answers Mia almost sprinted behind them. And in a few second she caught their pace and tapped on

Aamod's shoulder from behind. Aamod tuned and there was Mia in front of him. The shock of Mia being there was clearly visible on his face. The girl also turned and face Mia and she just looked into her eyes.

"Mia what are you doing here" Aamod couldn't hide his panic.

"I think I should ask that question to you, isn't it? You were supposed to be in Hyderabad, that is what you told me, the project is in the final stage and you have to be present there for last minute details and blah blah blah. I don't think we are in Hyderabad and clearly you are not finishing some last minute details. Who is this girl and what she is doing with you here? Are you here in town for all this time with this? What is going on here and for how long you are doing this?" Mia was shivering in anger and her eyes were now about to explode with tears. She was so much angry about her condition, about not knowing the facts, about Aamod's behavior with her for last few months. She just couldn't hold her anger, knowing that she was in public space.

"Mia, don't make scene over here, please let me explain to you everything. Let sit for a while and I will tell you everything." Aamod pleaded Mia, he was not sure what he was going to tell her, but at the moment he thought is the best to calm her down first.

"What scene, you have already made the scene Aamod. I am your wife Aamod, who has lost her memory, who is confused about where her life is going since she has lost almost eight year of her life, who need your support. And here you are having fun time with this person. You are avoiding responsibility of a husband and father just to keep this thing, I don't know who that is, and you are spending time with this person, which actually I should be spending with you. You have deserted me in most critical time of my life. When I needed your support the most. And you, do you know about me or you don't? And you didn't think about the consequences about being together with a married person? Of course not, girls like you never think about that, for you the only important thing is money, whoever throws money on you, you will go with them. I know this category of women and I am ashamed of those women who try to break the family, the house." Mia pointed out the last sentence towards Aarohi.

"I am not the one who is breaking your so called family, it's already broken. You don't remember that, so don't judge." Aarohi answered in calm tone with the pissed off look on her face.

Aamod squeeze Aarohi's hand, she looked at him and he shook his head requesting her to keep quiet. Mia saw that and she burst into tears which she had tried to keep at the edge for so long. She just couldn't accept that scene, which Aamod is in so much linked with someone else.

Aamod don't want to tell her the truth. He was so much confused about the situation. He never ever imagined that this would happen. Convincing Mia at this point was not possible for him. He asked her to get aside and let her sat on chair. He asked Aarohi to sit and pulled chair while calling Jay for help, but his phone was not reachable. After few minutes Mia got hold of herself. She looked at both of them and in calm voice she said "So have you both married?"

Aamod nodded in response.

"When?"

"Mia this is not the time to discuss all this, you are not in condition to understand the facts as you don't remember. Just be calm and take care of your health. You might not able to absorb the shock in this condition. This might be dangerous to you. When we asked doctor, he suggested us that if we told you all this, you might not accept it and it might worsen your condition. So we just decided to go with the flow." Aamod told the truth.

"So all these days when you were with me, you were married and that was the reason you kept distance from me, and I was cursing myself, that I must have done something wrong." Mia rub her hands on her face in disgrace.

"It was Jay's plan, that I should accompany you for some day till you partially recover. But it was very difficult for me to keep this from you. I was just following orders" Aamod tried to pacify Mia.

"Hmm. I am sorry Aarohi, you have gone through so much trouble for me and I was blaming you. But trust me, I wasn't aware anything of this. Please understood my position and forgive me. I am really very ashamed of what I said earlier." Mia was feeling so much guilty about the whole scene now

"Don't worry Mia, we don't mind it. We are sorry for all this, I never thought you will come here on your own. So I was careless, I never wanted you to learn it this way." Aamod console Mia, which Aarohi definitely didn't approve.

"Where is Neil, Mia? Are you here alone?" Aamod inquired.

"Oh my god. I asked Neil to wait for me at table. I hope he is still there. I have to rush there Aamod. I totally forgot about him, what is wrong with me, how can I forget about Neil? He must be scared by now" Mia said in frustration.

"Take it easy Mia, don't stress so much. He will be there, let's go and confirm. I am coming with you." Aamod got up and started walking with Mia and Aarohi followed them in confuse manner not knowing what to do.

Mia started running towards the direction where she and Neil were seated. Form a distance she noticed Neil was still enjoying his food and was at his comfort. She sighs in relief and rushed towards him.

"Hey ma, where is your coffee, you went to bring coffee and you forgot to get one?" Neil asked Mia in confused tone.

"Actually I stumble on you father" Mia replied. To that Neil gave a nervous look as what else must have happened. And he notice Aamod and Aarohi coming to their table. He waved to Aamod to go back, as he was not sure how Mia will react when she will notice Aarohi. Aamod nodded in assurance and came forward.

"Hey, are you ok."

"Yeah, what are you doing here dad?" Neil was not sure what to say

"That's a story to tell. How you guys have come here, do you want me to drop you back home, Mia?" Aamod asked Mia.

"We will managed Aamod, don't worry. We came by cab. And you don't have to come all the way there just drop us off. Will book cab while returning as well." Mia said in firm voice.

"You guys enjoy your day, we will now go back home, right Neil," Mia wanted head back home and away from Aamod as soon possible.

"Ok. Take care, will take your leave." Aamod noted that and waved good bye to them.

While going back Mia and Neil both were silent. Neil was not sure about what happened at the mall, and was nervous regarding Mia's health. This time he really wanted Jay to be present there to help him out of this situation. At this time Neil realized that he is really small to handle this. On the other side Mia was disturbed to the core after what happened in the mall, she was not able to understand that why Aamod did kept her in dark for so many days. Did he thought that she has weak mind, she could not digest the fact that he is married to someone else. What exactly has happened in all these years? Why I don't remember anything? She looked at Neil's frightened face, and gathered herself.

"Ma, you alright? Should we visit Doctor?"

"I am fine Neil, Don't worry. Now I just need to reach home and relax. No need to go to Doctor now." She smiled and pulled Neil towards her, giving assurance about her health. Neil felt relaxed and fall to sleep on her lap as he was tired too.

After reaching home, Mia made some sandwiches for them. Neil was exhausted from this day outing, he watched TV for some time and fall asleep on the couch. When Mia returned to living room after clearing the dishes and kitchen, she noticed Neil sleeping there. She didn't want to wake him up, she switched of the TV, lift Neil and tucked him to bed. She sat there running her hand though his hair for some time. She kissed on his forehead and muttered Good night to him while getting up, to her surprise Neil replied to her Good night, love you ma. She said love you too and while going out switched off the light. She kept the door of his room slightly open as always and went back to the living room.

There were loads of questions rising in her head about her lost memory, since Aarohi said those words to her. She felt so embarrassed about the whole situation that she still not able to get over it. Sleep was miles away from her. She tried to watch TV for some time, but nothing felt interesting to her. For an hour she kept on switching the channels and then felt tired of it and she switched off the TV, thinking when needed there is nothing to entertain. She sat there for a while thinking what next. Her laptop was lying there on the center table. She opened her laptop and started going through folders, thinking something might trigger her memory. And suddenly a photo popped up, with caption this day, last year. That photo was the same one of Jay and Neil enjoying on a beach, which was there in the Neil's bedroom. She clicked on that photo and the whole album opened. Mia started going through all the photos from that album. There were many photos of Jay and Neil and also of three of them. There was a photo of Mia and Jay holding hands and looking towards the setting sun. The photo was clicked from backside but Mia could make out that it was her and Jay. Mia sensed butterflies in her stomach when she saw that photo and her heart missed a bit. She wasn't sure what exactly that was, but yes she did felt something different while looking at that photo. She scrolled to the next photo and she was transfixed, it was photo in which Jay was carrying her is his hands and Mia had put her hand around his neck. That photo take her down to her memory lane.

They were on the beach of Daman. For so many days Neil was asking to go on beach, he wanted to make sand castle and wanted to play with waves, he was just constantly bragging about it. So Jay finally decided to take him to the beach. Jay and Neil spend the whole morning building the castle and it has turned out so well. Neil was very happy and excited about his castle. While they were building the castle, Mia was taking their photographs. Neil was so excited that he was constantly chatting about the castle.

"Jay uncle, when I grow up I will built the same castle as this one. And we all will go there to stay." Neil's excitement about castle was not reducing

"Ok, great. But built this castle some place near, otherwise how me and mom can come there to stay with you." Jay was also became the part of that play.

"Why, you can't come if the castle is not near our home" Neil was in doubtful mode

"How will we go to office then?" Neil asked him

"Arre Jay uncle, don't you understand, when we can built this big castle why you and mom need to work. We will have lot of money so you don't need to work." This was epic answer from Neil. From Neil's point of view, it is normal to have lot of money and then you don't have to work when you live in castle. So innocent thought it was.

"Oh, really, Then its fine. You built the castle and will come and stay with you" Jay was delighted to hear his innocent thoughts.

"And we will built a fountain in front of the castle. Or should we have a small pond with fishes. Or should we have pond and fountain both." Now the expansion of his castle has started.

"Ok, man. Take a breath. What you like the most. Then we can decide whether we should have fountain or a pond" Jay was so much thrilled to heat that question.

"I like both. I think we should have a pond with fishes in it and also a fountain in that pond" Neil had solution to all his problems it seems.

"Oh, that's great idea. In that way you can enjoy everything" Jay was now in mode of agreeing on everything with Neil.

"And where is my room, prince, where will I stay in you palace?" Mia interfere in their conversation.

"Mamma, you can choose your room, you have plenty of options." Neil left the choice on Mia.

"Hmm. I will prefer the room facing sea, I will love to watch the ocean at any time of day or night."

"We know" Jay and Neil smiled and gave high five to each other.

"Yeah I know that you know" Mia said this and started laughing.

Mia was watching Jay and Neil together building the castle. Neil was so happy with Jay. Mia for a while thought that Aamod was never able to spend such quality time with them. He never showed such interest in such things. Then she shook her head and tried to shove off thought about her past. Whatever happened in the past is happened. Now nothing to worry about it to make this moment sour. She again looked at them and smiled, in reply both waved to her and turned to work on their castle.

Jay has given that happiness, that peace to her and to Neil as well. The time of her separation and her divorce with Aamod was very tough for her. It was difficult to convey to Neil that his father and mother are not going to stay together. He was small but not that small that he didn't understood the tension between them. In some cases children think that they are the reason why their parents are not together. And that thought may hurt those children psychologically. Making them angry all the time or depressed or sad. But Jay helped Mia and Neil to pass through all that tough time. He was always there for them. At any time, any day. Jay was there like a steady light house guiding her always through those tough time psychologically. Making them feel that they don't need to face this alone at any point of time.

Mia's face lit up with this memory. The soothing thought about Jay take her soul to a peaceful place where she can rest herself in content. On that peaceful thought Mia fall asleep in wait of beautiful future which will kept her safe from the painful past.

#

Jay was disturbed at first on the camp site when he realized there was no network. But soon he engaged in so much activities at the camp that the network issue swept away from his mind. The Camping site was near a huge and beautiful lake surrounded by mountains and trees. Mountains were covered in green shawl of trees and the sky was clear blue. That azure blue color of sky was reflecting on the surface of the lake turning the lake into mesmerizing location. The clear sky, breezy and pleasant air, the greenery on mountains made that place a place of contemplation of self. Any person can spend infinite time in peace and tranquility at that location.

The setting of a tent was very difficult job but the kids and Jay enjoyed that much. After setting up the tent, they all had sandwiches that Sheena has packed for lunch. There were lot of other activities organized by that group like fishing, kayaking, and bird watching. While kayaking when Jay reached in the middle of the lake, he desperately missed Mia and decided to bring her and Neil along some time soon. He thought that Neil will definitely enjoy this ambience as he was aware about Neil's love for water.

Afternoon was completely occupied by those activities and by the time of sunset everyone was very hungry after all the activities. Everyone enjoyed the evening tea and Bhel party and now it was time for barbeque. The idea was everyone should be involved in barbeque, so someone was preparing the barbeque fire, someone was prepping the food and so on. Everybody was doing something or the other. When the sky got darker, they lit the campfire. It was time for dinner and it was very amusing experience to all of prepping food, barbequing. Sheena declared that she is not doing anything and needs to be served her place. She claimed that for all the time she serves and now it's time for her to be relaxed and get served.

After dinner Sheena insisted her younger daughter to play songs on her guitar.

"Sarah, we need to hear some songs from you" Sheena ordered her younger daughter.

"Mom, am I here to entertain you?" Sarah replied with her raised eyebrows.

"Hello, I don't pay for your guitar lessons, not to listen to that thing ever." Sheena gave her back

"But I didn't bought the guitar, so how you want me to play the songs now?" Sarah replied with narrowing her eyes.

"Ha Ha Ha, I was damn sure that you won't carry you guitar to escape from such situation. I knew it, but don't forget I am your mother, so I packed it, it is in the boot. Go get that and show us whether you really learnt anything after spending so much of money" Sheena laughed and that leave Sarah no choice but to play her guitar and she walked towards the car to fetch the guitar.

Sarah was good with guitar. She has made a good progress with her lessons and everyone enjoyed the songs she played. That changed the mood of everyone and then everyone contributed to that night and excitement of night got escalated. They all went to sleep after a while with great feeling.

Next day morning Jay got up early to watch Sunrise. Sheena also accompanied him for the view. They sat there watching the rising sun for as long as they can. The early morning breeze, the moist grass due to dew drops gave the atmosphere a fragrance which was supposed to be feel and not explain in words. That fragrance, mixed with wild flowers was yet a very different one. The smell of moist soil which was base of that fragrance mixed with light tones of wild flower and grass scent was difficult to match and filled in bottle. The both siblings were just sitting there and trying to fill their soul, their lungs, and their life with that fragrance, with that ambience.

After a while Sheena came out of the trance and looked around.

"Let's go dear. We have to pack up and leave for city today?" While taking look towards the beauty of nature Sheena exclaimed.

"Yep. We have to. I miss Mia so much here. She would have been so excited to see all this. She is a true nature lover. But because of this hectic city life we never able to visit such places." Jay gloomily said.

"Hmm, let her get out of this situation completely then will again plan for one camp night. Even Neil will enjoy with Sarah and Sameer." Sheena said in calm voice. To encourage him she said

"Let us race towards the camp site. Will see who reached there first." And started walking fast towards the camp site. Jay got up smiling and raced behind her.

When the car reached to the bottom of the hill they were camping, everyone's phone started beeping as they got the cellphone range and everyone started checking the phones.

"And now we lost contact with real people here" Sheena exaggerated in pale voice.

Jay also took out his phone and started going through messages. And he shouted loudly,

"Oh no, oh no, oh no." and he clasped is hand to forehead in annoyance.

"What happened?" Sheena asked him tension

"The one thing I was afraid of. It happened and I was not with her" Jay was upset

"Will you tell me exactly what happened? You are making me scared?" Sheena said in desperate voice.

"The thing I was most afraid of. I need to talk to Aamod first to understand what exactly has happened?" Jay said while dialing Aamod number.

"Will you tell me?" Sheena again requested. She wasn't sure about what has happened but if something must have happened to Mia, she couldn't have forgiven herself. Jay started to talk to Aamod and Sheena carefully tried to listen what they were talking.

"Hello Aamod, just received your messages. Can you please tell me what has happened?" Jay's voice was full of tension.

"Where were you? I tried to call you so many time, texted you but there was no reply from you?" Aamod was also looking tensed.

"I will explain that to you later. First you tell me how Mia is and what exactly has happened?" Jay was in no mood to explain anything but was more worried about Mia.

"Yesterday I and Aarohi went to mall for a movie. And all of sudden from nowhere Mia came in front of me. She was very angry and upset. She shouted at Aarohi and then Aarohi got upset told her about us. After that suddenly Mia became calm and silent and then she took off from the mall with Neil." Aamod tried to explain the story about what happened at the mall to Jay.

"Oh no. But why did you let her go on her own. I was not in town and even Anvi is. Mia is all alone. What must have going through her mind god only knows. Did you able to talk to her later?" After hearing the full scene of what happened at the mall, Jay got serious about Mia. Thousand things started running through his mind.

"Jay I requested her that I will drop her home. But she insisted on going alone. I couldn't force her.

And I texted her at night whether everything is alright or she need any help. But she replied with all ok, don't need to worry. What else I could have done. My only hope was you, so I called you. When I couldn't reach you I dropped the messages." Aamod tried to explain him everything.

"Hmm. All right. Ok. So she was fine till night we can say. I am on my way home. Will reach in next couple of hours. Meantime if required can you please assist her, if needed. Please." Jay requested Aamod.

"Of course. But get here as soon as possible. I am not sure if I can handle this situation anymore. I really can't." Aamod said in low voice.

"Yes I am trying to reach at the fastest way possible. Will keep in touch with you" Jay disconnected the phone and look gloomily towards Sheena.

"I am getting some idea from you conversation. But will you elaborate and tell me what has happened." Sheena was more worried after hearing the one side of conversation. Jay told her everything what Aamod told him.

"How much more time it is showing on the map?" Jay desperately asked

"About two hours. Now don't panic, try relax your mind and sit. Now whatever happened is happened. Will try to sort things out the most possible way." Sheena replied

"Hmm" Jay was restless but he was helpless as well. He texted Mia that he is on his way back to home. And will meet her as soon as he reached city.

#

Mia got up when Neelu rang the bell.

"Didi you were sleeping till now, everything is ok?' Neelu was surprised to see Mia sleeping till so late.

"Yes Neelu. I was awake till late last night, so my sleep was incomplete and I couldn't wake up." Mia yawned and turned her neck clockwise and counter clockwise. Sleeping on couch made her neck uneasy.

"Neelu, just gave me strong cup of coffee. And I will check on Neil. He must have tired from yesterday's outing." Mia tied her hair in bun and turned towards Neil's Bedroom.

After having the cup of coffee, Mia got her conscious sense and remembered everything happened yesterday. And the memory of Jay brought a smile on her face. She pick her phone up to check and aha, she didn't charge the phone yesterday and battery died. She plug the phone to charging and went to kitchen to instruct Neelu about directly making lunch. Neil was up and was informing in detail about the mall visit to Neelu. Looking at both of them engage in deep talks, Mia decided to take shower and went towards bathroom.

While taking shower the memory was constantly on her mind and she was blushing and smiling and was happy about that. That photo of her and Jay has triggered her memory. She understood why she had feelings about Jay and the guilt which she was facing earlier was completely vanished. She wanted to see Jay, to talk to him, to feel him once again. She wanted to take his hand and wanted to hug him tightly and rest her head on his chest. She wanted to feel his touch, to feel his breath, to engage his breath in hers. Just thinking about this she was blushing and smiling.

Mia finished her shower and changed. While getting ready she was humming. She felt like she has fallen in love just yesterday. It felt so great to be in love with the person who is also in love with you. Neelu entered the room worried and asked Mia

"Didi are you ok. Neil told me you saw Aamod sir with Aarohi madam yesterday."

"I am ok Neelu. It happened for better you know. Because of that I understood so many more things." Mia said in cheerful voice.

"I don't understand. But if you are fine then no problem. Do you want me to call Jay sir?" Neelu didn't felt assured but she didn't showed it.

"Don't worry Neelu. And that reminds me something." Mia patted on Neelu's shoulder and rush outside to check her phone. Neelu kept looking at her from behind with confused look on her face.

Mia switched on her phone and started going through messaged. Jay texted her that he is coming to meet her as soon as possible. It was an hour ago. So he will be here in an hour. She just texted him back OK, and didn't said a word. She wanted to surprise him. She wanted to see his expression when she will tell him about that memory. She didn't want to disclose that over a phone. So she decided to wait for him patiently. She informed Neelu that Jay will also be there for lunch.

#

Sheena dropped Jay at the entrance of the building.

"You sure you don't want me to come with you?" Sheena again asked Jay

"No. It's fine. She is OK. You all must be tired. Go home, get fresh and I will let you know everything. If I need you I will definitely call you. So just go." Jay waved bye to all and rushed towards the building.

Bell rang and Neelu almost ran to open the door. Neelu open the door and look worriedly at Jay. Jay just raised his eyebrows and asked Neelu about situation silently. Neely raised her shoulder as don't know and let him in.

"Hi" Jay greeted

"Hi, how was your camping?" Mia showed no sign of her feeling in voice.

"Good. How was your weekend?" Jay was trying to open up the topic.

"Good. Neil will give you in detail story of our weekend." Mia smiled and said.

Jay was confused, how come she is so calm and not angry about hiding things from her. He was not sure how to ask her about Aamod and Aarohi. So he tuned to Neil

"Hey buddy, how was your weekend?"

"Jay uncle I am not talking to you? Why didn't you took me with you for camping?" Neil was still not forgot that.

"Will go next Saturday for sure? I miss you so much there." Jay assured Neil about camping

"Promise"

"Promise, Now tell me about your weekend." Jay wanted to know about the scene at the mall.

"Jay, let's eat lunch first. I am starving. Neelu, let's set the table. Neil go and wash your hands. Jay do you want to freshen up" Mia ordered everyone. Jay nodded and turned towards bathroom.

Jay was not sure about what's going on in Mia's mind. He was expected her to be angry. He thought she would start questioning him as soon as he entered. She will scold him for keeping her in dark about her life, about her husband. But here the scene was totally different. There is absolutely no sign of anger. Mia was as normal as she was always. Jay was confused and scared as he was not able to understand what will happen next.

While having lunch Neil told the whole episode of how he enjoyed at the mall, and how they came across Aarohi and Aamod. But Mia showed zero interest in that. She was all concentrated in lunch and then Jay thought may be Mia don't want to discuss about Aamod as she don't think I am part of her life. I am just her Business Partner, nothing more. Why would anyone discuss their personal life with their Business Partner? That thought made Jay upset. He wasn't sure now how he would tell Mia that she is love of his life. That he don't want to stay away from her anymore. He doesn't want spent a moment without her. Till now she was in impression that she is married to Aamod, but now as she is aware of her divorce how she will react towards me? What if she never remember about me? What if as Dr. Patel said, she will not accept me as her life partner and decides to live alone? Oh god please help me. I don't want to be parted with her. All this thoughts made him so nervous that Jay couldn't hide his emotions.

"What happened Jay, are you alright? You didn't look good" Mia immediately understood the changes on Jay's face.

"No. I am ok. Just don't have appetite." Jay couldn't say anything about his thoughts.

"Hmm. You must have ate something midway while coming here." Mia said

They finished lunch and Neil felt sleepy, Mia put him to sleep. Neelu also finished dishes and left.

Mia picked up the photo of Neil and Jay from Daman from Neil's Room and came outside.

"Jay, when did this picture is taken?" Mia asked Jay. Jay took that photo and kept glazing that photo. How he can forget those beautiful memory. But what is the point now. He just nodded

"It has been clicked in Daman last year, this day. Do you remember?" Mia looked into Jay's eye and asked him

"How do you know?" Jay eyes were wide to hear this.

"I recollect. Why didn't you told me about us Jay. Why did you kept me in dark about Aamod and Aarohi?" Mia asked him in hurt voice.

"But how, what made you remember us?" Jay was still in shock and wasn't believed what he was listening.

"Yesterday after returning from mall, I wasn't sure what to do? As I was not aware about "us", I was so much confused to whom should I talked to? My mind was just circling along that scene I created at the mall, and I was feeling sort of guilty. I opened Laptop and started searching something to past the time and suddenly this photo popped up, reminding this day last year. And puff, it reminded me about us. So I went through some more photos of that day, which you have hidden on my laptop. Why you didn't want me to see those photos?" Mia laughed and said that in one breath.

"I did wanted you to remember it. If I would have told you, then you might have understood and accepted it. But what about the feelings, the love, I would have missed that. I wanted to tell you everything but I wanted you to feel that as well Mia. Only God knows how much I wanted to tell you that what you meant to me, how much I love you, how you are essence of my life. But just speaking of the words wouldn't have brought those feelings." Jay sighed and continued "These last couple of months were very hard for me. You, the love of my life was in front of me but I was not allowed to touch you, to take you in my arms, to kiss you, to give you assurance that everything is going to be alright, for that matter whatever happens, I am always there for you. Mia I am so happy to that you got your memory back. I am thankful to god for giving me my Mia back." Tears started rolling down from Jay's eyes. He took her hand in his one hand and stroke his fingers on her cheek and push back her strands of hair behind her ear.

Looking into his eyes Mia said, "Jay, when I was going through those Daman photos yesterday, all of a sudden, I remembered your touch, your warn breath and your love. And then understood your behavior towards me. Somewhere deep in my mind I know that I was in love with you, that is the reason why I was more comfortable when you were around. I remembered all your likes, dislikes, habits. But I was not sure why I remember those."

"So do you remember everything?" Jay whispered in Mia's ear.

"Not everything Mister. But I remember enough. Now instead of wasting time on remembering the past, I think we should invest in making more new memories. Right" Mia was blushing with the closeness of Jay

"You are always right my dear, let's make new memories"

Jay hold Mia's face in his hand and kissed her. He picked her up and headed towards bedroom. They were now ready to make new memories and embrace the chance, life has offered.

The Beginning….

www.ingramcontent.com/pod-product-compliance
Lightning Source LLC
LaVergne TN
LVHW041708070526
838199LV00045B/1257